The Cats that Cooked the Books

Karen Anne Golden

Copyright

This book or eBook is a work of fiction.

Atlantic City, New Jersey, and Nyack, New York, are real places. The town of Erie is not. The characters I create do not exist, nor have they ever lived in these cities.

Names, characters, places and incidents are products of my imagination or are used fictitiously. Any resemblance to actual events, locales, persons or cats, living or dead, is entirely coincidental.

Edited by Vicki Braun

Book cover concept by Karen Anne Golden

Graphic design by Rob Williams

    Copyright © 2020 Karen Anne Golden

      All rights reserved.

ISBN: 9798630578068

Dedication

For my husband Jeff

Table of Contents

Introduction 1
Chapter One 3
Chapter Two 8
Chapter Three 24
Chapter Four 42
Chapter Five 56
Chapter Six 59
Chapter Seven 72
Chapter Eight 91
Chapter Nine 95
Chapter Ten 104
Chapter Eleven 121
Chapter Twelve 127
Chapter Thirteen 136
Chapter Fourteen 143
Chapter Fifteen 154
Chapter Sixteen 161
Chapter Seventeen 163
Chapter Eighteen 175
Chapter Nineteen 178
Chapter Twenty 188
Chapter Twenty-One 190
Chapter Twenty-Two 210
Chapter Twenty-Three 226
Chapter Twenty-Four 249
Chapter Twenty-Five 253

Coincidence

An occasion when two or more things happen at the same time, especially in a way that is unexpected or unlikely.

Cambridge Dictionary

Introduction

Katherine "Katz" Cokenberger, a thirty-one-year-old heiress, didn't always live in the small town of Erie, northwest of Indianapolis, Indiana. She grew up in Brooklyn, went to NYU, and became a computer professional. After inheriting money from a great aunt, Katherine moved to the Midwest to take care of a pink Victorian mansion and an Abyssinian cat. *Easy peasy*, she thought. She loved cats and already had three Siamese, so what was one more? But in the words of her late mother, "Be careful what you wish for, because the outcome may not match up to your dreams." Soon after moving to the quaint town, Katherine's pink mansion became known as a murder magnet because of the number of crimes that would be committed there.

Putting aside the mansion's not-so-stellar reputation, Katherine counted her many blessings. She'd married the love of her life, Jake Cokenberger, who was a history professor at the City University. The couple's feline family had increased to seven: six Siamese and one ruddy-ticked Abyssinian. However, none of their cats was your garden-variety house cat. Each feline had unique abilities beyond the realm of the everyday cat. Siamese littermates Scout and Abra performed a macabre death dance and had the strange ability to predict murder. Iris and Abby stole evidence from criminals and hid it in a wingback chair, then retrieved it when an alert investigator was around. And most extraordinary of all was the cats' habit of clandestinely surfing the Internet to provide clues to solving crimes.

Katherine's best friend Colleen Murphy moved from New York to Erie to go to college in the city, and recently married Jake's cousin, Daryl Cokenberger, a deputy sheriff from the neighboring county. Ex-con Stevie Sanders was getting on with his life, raising a teenaged daughter.

And Chief London could relax because a capital crime hadn't been committed in Erie for a few years.

Until a blast from the past stormed in, leaving tragedy in its wake.

Chapter One

Far Away from Erie, Indiana
Atlantic City, New Jersey

Rose Martinez, an Atlantic City casino bookkeeper, made her way across the gaming floor. She came in early to finish up an accounting project she'd started the day before. She wasn't surprised by the meager number of players at the slot machines. On a weekday, at six in the morning, it wasn't usual to have a full crowd of easy targets — busy losing their money — as she called them to her co-workers. As she walked, she didn't notice the man following her. She was distracted by the loud music playing overhead and the constant din of slot machines, each blaring out its own kind of music.

Rose headed to the refreshment kiosk to fill her office mug to take upstairs where she worked. She adjusted her leather tote bag, and leaned in to press the diet soda button. She overfilled her mug, and the drink splashed on her white suit blouse. "Dang, I have to get this stain out before it sets," she said, annoyed. She spotted the nearby restroom, set her mug on the kiosk counter, and darted into the ladies' room. She positioned her roomy bag next to the sink.

While she yanked paper towels out of the dispenser, a man came up from behind, grabbed her by the hair, and held her head back. She brought her hands up to disengage the attacker's grip, but he was much stronger than she was. He yanked her hair even harder. "Gimme your phone," he demanded.

"Why do you want my phone?" she gasped.

"Shut up! Give it to me," he repeated, pushing her face down in the ceramic bowl of the sink.

"Get off of me. How am I supposed to give it to you, when you won't let me get in my bag," she said, struggling to breathe.

He wrenched her head back and pushed her to the floor.

Rose fell hard on her knees. She winced with pain. She sat down, turned to face her attacker, and took a good look at him. She'd never seen him before. She didn't think he was one of the players she'd just seen on the gaming floor, because he was too well-dressed. He wore a black business suit with a crisp white shirt and black tie. She couldn't understand why a man so impeccably attired would want to harm her.

The man reached over, grabbed the bag and dumped the contents in the sink. Fumbling through the personal contents — wallet, comb, hand sanitizer, and a wallet-sized photo album of Rose's grandchildren, he barked angrily, "Where is it?"

Rose rubbed the back of her head. "Who *are* you?"

"I said, where is it?" he commanded loudly.

"It's . . . it's," she stuttered. "It's not there."

The man eyed her suspiciously. "Are you freakin' nuts? Just tell me where it is?"

"Give me a second to catch my breath."

The man walked over to her and drew his fist back like he was going to hit her.

"It's in my left pocket."

"Get up," he said, extending his hand to help her to her feet. He frisked her and found the phone. He grabbed her right hand and forced her thumb onto the home button to unlock it. Scrolling down her recent calls list, he looked up. "What did you talk to Emma about?"

"Emma?"

"Emma Thomas. You work with her."

"Oh, that Emma. She called to tell me she'd quit without notice. I told her that was a terrible idea because she wouldn't get a reference for her next job."

"Stop," he said, putting his hand up. "I know she quit yesterday. Did she tell you where she was going?"

"I got the impression she didn't have a job to go to."

"Listen, stupid, I asked where she was going?"

"Well, I assume she went home. I hardly know Emma. Why would she tell me this kind of personal information?"

The man eyed her suspiciously. He scrolled down several lines of recent phone calls, but only one of them was Emma's. He tapped the number. A "call failed" message appeared on the screen.

He asked again gruffly, "Did she tell you where she was going?"

"No, she did not!" she answered adamantly. "I'm telling you the truth."

"You better not be lying to me," he said in a threatening voice.

"I beg your pardon. Lying?" Rose huffed. "I've done a good job for this casino, and I've never been accused of lying. I will tell you one thing, Mister, that is the absolute truth. I'm heading straight upstairs and I'm telling my manager, that you, whoever you are, attacked me. And I hope if you work here, you'll get fired! You can't go around attacking employees."

"Is that a fact?" he said, heading for the door.

"How about I sue you for assault? I'm calling Security right now and tell them you hit me!"

"I *am* Security, you stupid woman."

Chapter Two

Mid-July in Erie

Daryl's and Colleen's Wedding Reception

Late Saturday Afternoon

Jake Cokenberger drove his Jeep Wrangler off the paved highway onto a gravel drive and to the barn where a wedding reception was being held for newlyweds Daryl and Colleen. One week before, the couple had been married in Queens, New York, and afterward attended a reception held by Colleen's Mum. Many of Daryl's relatives and friends didn't have the money to fly to New York and stay in a hotel, so the solution to the problem was to have two receptions. The Indiana reception was being hosted by Daryl's side of the family, which included family members from all over the Midwest.

Katherine rode shotgun. "I didn't realize the infamous wedding barn was on a gravel road."

Jake hit a deep rut, and the Jeep bounced.

"Whoa, there, cowboy, slow down," she advised.

Jake pulled into the gravel parking lot, which was full of pickup trucks.

"Are we late?"

"No, we're right on time," Jake answered.

"Why is everyone standing outside?"

"They're waiting for Daryl and Colleen to show up. Daryl's driving the old '67 Impala and wanted to make a fun entrance."

"Okay, I got it. I don't think Colleen is aware of this or she would have told me."

Jake parked, then walked over and opened Katherine's passenger door. She struggled to climb out of the Jeep. Her short calico dress hiked up.

Jake admired. "Nice legs, I mean kicks." He grinned mischievously.

"Quit it," she scolded. "I can't get out. My dang cowboy boot is hung up on something. I'm stuck."

Jake reached in and unhitched the problem boot, then helped Katherine out of the Jeep. Before he set her down, he kissed her hard on the lips. "Just thought I'd get a kiss in before the soiree."

Katherine giggled. "A barn soiree. That's new."

The couple walked to the front of the barn and joined the group standing outside. Grandpa Cokenberger came over and gave Katherine his signature hug.

"I've forgotten what a hearty hugger you are," she said, laughing.

"There they are," someone yelled from the back of the group.

Daryl slowly drove his black Impala and parked it in front of the barn. The vintage car door squeaked when he climbed out. He was dressed like Jake — blue jeans, white shirt, and cowboy string tie. He walked around the car to open Colleen's door, but Grandpa had beat him to it. The elderly gentleman was attired the same way.

Grandpa extended his hand and helped Colleen out. "You're just about the purdiest gal I've ever seen," he said.

"Who's the purdiest?" Colleen asked with a glint in her eye.

"My wife, of course," Grandpa beamed.

Colleen wore a short, white lacy bridal dress. Her long red hair was styled in a wavy mass of curls. On her feet, she sported a pair of pointy-toed cowboy boots. She caught Katherine's eye and pointed toward her boots.

Katherine brought her hand up to her mouth to keep from laughing. Colleen was never one for boots, let alone cowboy boots.

Cora Cokenberger, Jake's mother and co-planner of the reception, said in a low, snippy voice to her sister, June (aka Daryl's mom), "I told her not to wear them boots."

June shushed her. "On this day, a bride can wear whatever she wants."

Cora gave a pinched-up facial expression.

Two men in their twenties, the Cokenberger twins from Ohio, were dressed in matching red plaid shirts with suspenders, blue jeans and cowboy boots. They slid open the barn door, and motioned for the bridal couple to go inside where the band was playing the wedding march on their fiddles and upright bass.

Daryl took Colleen's hand and they made their way to the bridal table next to a small stage. Katherine and Jake followed, and were surprised that the bridal table was a two-seater and didn't include chairs for them.

"Cuz, your table is right there," Daryl said, pointing to the round table close-by.

The large round table comfortably seated eight, and was appropriately appointed with a crisp, red and white tablecloth. The centerpiece was a bottle of champagne, sitting in a wood crate along with flutes. The crate also held non-alcoholic sparkling wine for non-drinkers and a giant pitcher of sweet tea. Next to the pitcher were eight Mason jars.

Jake held Katherine's chair and she sat down.

Katherine asked, "What's with the jars?"

Jake sat down and grabbed two jars. He poured tea into each, and handed Katherine her glass. "Well, shucks pumpkin, country folk can't afford no fancy glasses. We have to eat a lot of canned tomaters to git these jars."

Katherine poked him in the ribs. "Why shucks, I had no idea," she mimicked.

Jake grinned and made fun of her fake country accent. "You sound like you're from Brooklyn."

"That's because I am," she smirked.

Inside the barn, the tables quickly filled up with Jake's large family. Cokey, Margie, and their two teenaged children, Shelly and Tommy, sat at the table next to them, and were joined by Jake's parents, Johnny and Cora, and Daryl's parents, Walton and June. Jake's grandparents sat at a table with family members from Ohio. Daryl's law enforcement cronies sat at another table, and were joined by Daryl's boss, Sheriff Johnson.

Since Colleen's Mum had hosted a reception after the couple's formal wedding in Queens, none of Colleen's relatives were there, only her closest friend in the world, Katherine, who was more like a sister than a friend.

Jake noted that no one had joined them at their table. "Maybe we'll have it all to ourselves."

"Don't spread out too soon. Check out the place cards."

Jake looked at the folded wedding card next to him. "Oh, you won't believe who I'll be sitting next to?"

"Who?"

"Our old friend Detective Martin."

As if on cue, Linda Martin, detective with the Indiana State Police, walked in, arm-in-arm with Mark Dunn, Katherine's former estate attorney. They were followed by Chief London and his wife, Connie. They both walked over to the table. Jake and Katherine stood up to greet them.

Katherine said excitedly to Mark and Linda, "It's been way too long since I've seen you two." She hugged them, then said to the chief and Connie, "I'm so glad we're all sitting at the same table."

Connie, attired in a red and white gingham dress reminiscent of the famous Minnie Pearl's signature costume, said to Katherine, "I love your dress. It's perfect for a reception in a barn. I mean . . . I mean," she stuttered, "I meant it as a compliment."

Katherine smiled. "I love yours, too." She bit her tongue to avoid admitting she wasn't a fan of the imposed dress code, but she had to comply with Cora's and June's wishes. And then pinched herself, because it could have been one of the dresses Cora favored that looked like it came off the set of *Gone with the Wind*.

Everyone sat down.

Jake noted, "We have two more seats at this table. I wonder who else is coming?"

The chief reached over and picked up the place card. "Stevie and Salina Sanders."

Jake eyed Katherine curiously, and each silently questioned why Cora would seat Stevie up front with a family whose majority of members didn't care for him.

A very shy fifteen-year-old, with long blond braids, walked in. She wore a calico skirt with a western blouse. She nervously eyed the tables for her place. Cokey's and Margie's daughter, Shelly, stood up and yelled, "Salina, over here." Shelly and Salina were thick as thieves.

When Katherine saw Salina arrive, she rose and rushed over to her. "Hi, Salina. You're sitting at my table."

"KC, Dad couldn't come," she said in a quiet voice, not offering an excuse.

Katherine didn't ask for one. She suspected Stevie would feel awkward attending the reception. And since the false rumor of their having a passionate affair, she hadn't seen Stevie very much — almost as if he was avoiding her.

"Salina, over here," a very excited Shelly yelled again.

"KC, is it okay if I sit by Shelly?"

"Yes, of course. Besties always sit together," Katherine winked. "I'll catch up with you later." She returned to her seat.

The crowd got very lively and were clinking their mason jars with their knives. Daryl promptly kissed Colleen. Then a loud *Yee-haw* resounded off the walls of the rustic-paneled barn.

The guests at the table exchanged pleasantries while they waited for their turn at the buffet table.

Mark said, "Well, Katz, I seem to think wherever you go there's some kind of adventure."

"Oh, you must have heard the latest about Colleen's and my trip to the Indiana Dunes," she said, then changed the subject. She didn't want to get into the topic of how strange events followed her wherever she went or how her house, the pink mansion, was a murder magnet. Instead, she asked, "How are you liking your job in Indy?"

"I made partner at the firm," Mark beamed.

A round of congratulations circled the table.

Katherine said, "Jake has some good news, too."

"What's that?" Mark asked.

"You're looking at the new department head," Jake announced.

Linda asked, "History, right?"

Jake smiled.

Mark spoke, "Linda and I have some great news also."

"Yes, we do," Linda said with a grin. "We're getting married in the fall."

"That's wonderful," Jake said.

"Congratulations," everyone said at the same time.

"Is the wedding going to be in Indy or Erie?" Chief London asked.

"In Indy. You're all invited, so be looking for your save-the-date postcards."

Connie, an avid gardener, interjected, "Katz, come over to my house soon. I'm dividing my daylilies."

"Yes, I definitely will."

Jake chuckled. "Katz has planted so many daylilies at our house, she needs another acre or two of land."

"I have not," Katherine disagreed.

Connie laughed.

Chief London asked, "How are the cats?"

Jake answered, "Our cats are just fine."

"How's the Abyssinian? What's her name again?" Linda inquired.

"Abigail, but we call her Abby," Katherine said.

"Oh, that's right."

Mark asked Linda, "How do you know her?"

"Well, let's just say Abby has expensive tastes."

"How's that?" he asked.

"She likes to play hockey with expensive objects."

Katherine giggled. "Especially, rare, brown diamonds."

Katherine was glad everyone knew what she was referring to and didn't have to mention how Abby had pilfered a diamond from a friend's purse, and used it as a hockey puck for days before she dropped it on Detective Martin's foot.

"Here's a little piece of trivia," Mark said. "I drove Katherine's late great aunt to Wisconsin to pick up Abby."

"I remember you telling me that. I'm so happy you did," Katherine said.

The evening wore on with too much eating, drinking, dancing, and having a wonderful time. Katherine rose from her chair and walked over to Salina's table. She asked the teen, "Do you have a ride home?"

Salina nodded and said in a happy voice, "I'm staying with Shelly tonight."

Margie piped in, "Yes, a sleepover. Cokey and I'll take her home."

"Oh, okay. That works. How have you been, Margie?" Katherine asked.

"I have a new remodeling job downtown. Do you remember where the *Buy it Here* antique store was, next to the Erie Hotel?"

Katherine nodded. "Several weeks ago, I saw the 'For Sale' sign in the window. I'm glad it sold. I was worried no one would buy it because of how shabby it looked on the outside."

"Shabby on the inside too," Margie added.

Katherine eyed her table. Jake stood up and motioned her to the dance floor. She nodded and said, "I'll see you later. I can't deny a handsome man a dance."

"Who me?" Cokey teased.

Katherine winked. "No, not you, the other handsome Cokenberger."

Close to midnight, Daryl and Colleen stood up and walked to each table and thanked everyone for coming. They stopped at the head table first.

"Are you all having a good time?" Daryl asked.

"Yes, we are," they said in unison. A well-meant round of congratulations was voiced to the happy couple.

Colleen stood behind Katherine, and bent down and said, "What did you think of our grand entrance in the Impala?"

"I think it was so romantic. I remember the first time you met Daryl."

Colleen smiled. "You were dating Jake. Jake introduced me to Daryl. The four of us were going to a fish fry and Daryl drove."

"And?" Katherine prompted.

"I thought it was so cool that he had a classic car. It was love at first sight."

Daryl picked up on the end of the conversation. He reached over and hugged Colleen. "I heard that. Did you marry me for my car?"

Colleen belted out a loud laugh. "Come on, handsome. We have other tables to go to. Katz, I'll catch you later," she said, leaving.

After the proud couple walked over to the next table, Katherine lightly grabbed Jake's arm and whispered in his ear, "Who's that guy back there?"

"What guy? The place is crawling with guys?"

"The big one standing at the entrance."

"I don't see anyone."

"Geez, look closer. He looks like Luca Brasi."

"From the *Godfather* movie?"

"Yes, waiting to offer his wedding congratulations or something."

"Oh, that's Ted," Jake laughed. "He's a jack of all trades. Today, he's a bouncer."

"What? He works for the wedding barn people?"

"Not just the barn people," Jake teased. "He works for anyone who has odd jobs to do. Daryl gave him a few extra bucks to watch out for anyone looking like they're packing shaving cream."

Katherine scrunched up her face in disbelief. "Shaving cream? Why would anyone bring shaving cream to a reception?"

"Daryl doesn't want anyone messing with the Impala."

"What does his car have to do with it?"

"He doesn't want folks to write "Just Married" or some other prank message on his car. Shaving cream can permanently discolor the paint, and because the Impala has been painted before, Daryl doesn't want to take the chance."

"Seriously?"

"Yep, seriously."

Daryl and Colleen returned and assumed their places at the bridal table.

Someone sitting at a table close to where the bouncer stood, screamed, "Look out! A rat!"

The guests stopped talking. A big hush fell over the rowdy crowd.

A very proud, rotund, ginger cat strolled in, with something dangling from his mouth — a very dead field mouse.

One of the members of the band sang into the microphone, "Who let the cat in? Meow. Meow."

The cat was oblivious to the crowd. He trotted down the aisle between two rows of tables, jumped up on the stage, deposited the mouse, and then made a beeline back to the door. The bouncer graciously opened it for the feline, who left with his tail hiked straight up in the air, then Ted called after the cat, "Mouser, git back in the truck!"

One of the catering staff grabbed a napkin and went over and picked up the mouse.

"Eww," Shelly and Salina shouted at the same time, then the crowd started to laugh.

Colleen called over to Katherine, "Is that considered good or bad luck?"

"It's good luck!" Katherine grinned, not sure if that was the correct answer, but the right answer to her superstitious friend.

Colleen snickered. "Only in Indiana."

The guests started clinking their glasses again. Colleen leaned into Daryl and said, "My lips are numb."

Daryl kissed her on the nose. "Mine are, too. How about we blow this popsicle stand?"

Chapter Three

Emma Thomas, former cat wrangler for a famous magician, vet tech major and graduate with an associate's degree in bookkeeping, got off the bus in Nyack, New York. She walked several blocks, then stopped to make sure no one was following her. Then she crossed the street and backtracked a block. She hailed a cab, which drove ten blocks to where her grandmother owned a Victorian house along the Hudson River. Paying the cab driver in cash, she got out and walked a block in the opposite direction. When the cab was out of sight, she turned and hurried to her grandmother's. Now, a little out of breath from the long diversionary hike, she stood outside the back door and hesitated to go inside. She didn't want to face the sad news that her beloved Grammy was dying.

The caregiver, Nancy, was in the kitchen and saw Emma through the window. She opened the door, "Hello, love," she said. "Come in. Make yourself at home. Pearl wants some soup, so I popped out here to make it."

Emma walked in and put her Vera Bradley satchel purse on the kitchen counter. "Tomato Bisque, right?"

"Her favorite."

"How is she today?"

Nancy didn't answer for a few seconds, then said, "Not good. You better brace yourself, dear," she paused, then said in a sad voice, "Ms. Pearl is not long for the world."

Emma brought her hand up to her lip and covered her mouth to stifle the sob that was growing deep inside her. A tear fell from her eye. She wiped it off before it ran down her cheek.

Nancy poured the can of soup into a large cup and placed it in the microwave. "Sweetie, I'll let you compose yourself before you go in. I know you don't want to upset her."

Emma nodded, took a deep breath, then walked down the hall to her grandmother's bedroom.

Pearl was sitting up on an ornate walnut Rococo bed, with a tall headboard. She had several pillows propped up so she could see the document she held in her hand. Her boyfriend Lawrence sat on a chair beside the bed.

When the door opened, Pearl looked up, surprised. "Emma, my sweet girl, come in. What a welcome surprise. I didn't know you were coming."

Emma walked over and took her grandmother's hand. "It's good to see you."

Lawrence stood up and hugged Emma. "Long time, no see."

"How are you?" Emma asked Lawrence, then regretted asking such an insensitive question. She thought, *Of course he's not okay. The love of his life is passing away.*

Pearl said in a weak voice, "Pull up that chair in the corner and sit close to me. We need to talk business. I need to tell you some legal things. I don't want you to interrupt me because I don't want to think about it too much. Okay?"

"Sure," Emma said, drawing up the chair and sitting down.

Lawrence started to leave, but Pearl called him back. "I want you to be in on this meeting, too."

He walked back and sat back down in his chair. "Okay, dear."

Emma said lightly, trying to change the depressing tone of the conversation to a sunnier one, "Official meeting, huh?" She smiled. "Should I take notes?"

Pearl chuckled, then returned her gaze to the document she held in her hand. "I was going over this with Lawrence. You came in just at the right moment. I've made a numbered list. Emma your name is on my checking and savings account. When I pass, my lawyer will take care of removing my name. Every nickel and dime in that account will go to you, honey, including what's in there now and what I will get for my house."

"Grammy—" Emma started to interrupt.

Pearl put her hand up. "Stop, let me finish. I put my house up for sale and it sold in two days. Seems there're a lot of folks out there who love Victorian homes."

Emma was shocked. "I had no idea you were going to sell this house. Why didn't you tell me?"

"Because you would have tried to talk me out of it."

Emma agreed. "Probably."

"It makes perfect sense to sell it now. That way you don't have to mess with it. Okay, next on my list. While you're here, I want you to go through the house and pick out what furniture you want. I need to know lickety-split because in two weeks there's going to be an auction."

"Auction? Where?"

"Somewhere in Manhattan at one of those swanky auction houses. Lawrence is taking care of that. Right, dear?"

"Yes, I have that covered," he said in a sad voice.

"Emma, I want you to understand that I want Lawrence to have the money made at the auction."

"Oh, Grammy, that's a wonderful idea, but I don't really want any of the furniture. I'd like the family photos, things like that, but not the furniture."

Lawrence stood up, "I really must go now. I have several errands to run. Pearl, do you want me to bring you back anything from the deli?"

"Yes, that's a great idea. Bring back something for dinner, so we can sit in the dining room like old times."

Lawrence picked up Pearl's hand and kissed it, then he left.

Pearl returned to the topic at hand. "Are you sure you don't want some of the furniture? What about your bedroom set? You've had it since you were a teenager."

"No, thanks, Grammy."

Pearl took a deep breath, then asked, "How have you been? Are you still working at the casino, oh, forgive me for not remembering its name?"

Emma shook her head. "I'm not working there anymore."

"Really? That's news to me," Pearl said, stunned. "When did you quit?"

Emma shrugged her shoulders and remained quiet for a moment. She wanted to say that in the last twenty-four hours she'd been a very busy girl. For starters, she'd quit her job without notice. She'd left her fiancé, Ray Russo. She went to the bank and withdrew her entire savings account, only leaving a few hundred in the checking. After that, she used her key to the joint-owned safe deposit box she shared with Ray, and withdrew another $250 thousand in cash (his money or the mob's money, she wasn't sure which), and a pink USB flash drive.

Her plan had been to open the deposit box and take out half the cash, but she got a little greedy. She knew Ray had tons of money stashed away, which she wasn't privy to. Finding the flash drive was a surprise. She'd never seen it in the box before. It was lying on the bottom in a manila envelope with a metal clasp. Curious like a cat, she'd opened it. A note was folded inside. She'd pulled it out and read it. Written in red ink: *Guard this with your life. It's the complete ledger of our operations. Signed Marcel.* She'd peered into the envelope and saw the flash drive, then tipped the envelope and the flash drive slid out. It was labeled: AR. *AR*, she'd thought, then a light bulb went on in her head— *accounts receivable.* She'd slipped the flash drive in her purse, put the note back in the envelope, re-clasped it, and returned it to the box. She didn't have a clue what was on it, but she'd make it a point to find out.

Pearl asked a second time, "When did you quit your job?"

"Yesterday."

"Why?"

"I have other plans."

"What about your fiancé? What does he think of your plans?"

"Seriously, Grammy, I don't give a damn."

"What?"

"I left Ray."

"Oh, my!" Pearl said, shocked. "Why?"

"Because he's a crook. I'll spare you the sordid details."

"What did he say when you told him you were leaving him?"

"I didn't have to tell him. I got lucky."

"How is that?"

"Yesterday afternoon, when I came home to our apartment—"

Pearl cut her off. "You said *our* apartment. Honey, I didn't know you lived with Ray."

"I'm a big girl now, Grammy. It was cheaper to share expenses. Why maintain two residences when you can share one?" Emma knew her grandmother didn't approve. Back in her day, women didn't share apartments with men unless they were married.

"Go on."

"As soon as I walked in the door, my cell rang. It was Ray, a very annoyed Ray. Seems he was in a bit of trouble and needed me to bail him out of jail."

"Jail?"

"I told him I had a horrible headache and that I'd get one of his friends to do it."

"What did Ray do to land in jail?"

"Oh, he assaulted a New Jersey police officer over a speeding ticket. After Ray finished screaming at me—"

"Screaming?"

"Yeah! He went ballistic when I said I couldn't bail him out."

"What did you do?"

"I held the line until he calmed down, then he said I could call his friend, Marcel. I said I would, but you know what?" Emma asked, smirking. "The beauty of it is, I didn't call Marcel, and for all I know, Ray's still in jail."

"Oh, my goodness."

"Serves him right," Emma said.

Pearl shook her head, "I hope he doesn't come after you."

"If he does, he won't find me."

"Why is that?"

"Grammy, I came here to tell you I'm moving. I bought a three-story building."

"A building? A whole building?" Pearl asked with interest.

"Well, it's sort of like a row house connected to other buildings on a main street. It has enough room on the first floor for a small café."

"A café?"

"I want to open a coffee bar in a small town."

"Here in New York, or New Jersey?"

"Not, exactly. I can't afford anything here. Everything listed on the real estate websites were too expensive for me."

"So, where's the building? Row house?"

"I'll get to that part in a minute," Emma said, smiling. "I found a business that used to be an antique store. I'm having the first floor remodeled to be a quaint, little coffee shop where I'll serve different blends of coffee, tea and maybe a light fare of cookies and muffins," she explained dreamily.

"I didn't see a deduction in our checking account. Did you get a mortgage?"

"I bought it in cash. My cash. Sight unseen."

"Congratulations, sweetheart. This is great news. I want to hear more about it."

"There were two real estate contenders: one in the South and the other one in the Midwest. The one in Midwest was a better deal because the asking price was lower than the one in the South. What's really amazing is that I can live above the coffee shop. The second floor has a living room, kitchen, half bath and a flex room. The third floor has two spacious bedrooms and a full bathroom."

"Sweetie, it sounds perfect, but the Midwest is a big area. Where in the Midwest?"

Emma didn't answer the question, but went on describing the three-story building, "It was advertised as a storefront because the site where it's located is surrounded by other businesses, which, and you will love this part, are historic buildings on the National Register for Historic Places."

"It sounds wonderful, dear, but where? You didn't tell me where? I'll need your address."

"I'll call and give it to you later this week."

"Well, promise me that once you've moved to your new place, you can adopt a cat or two — maybe a pair of Siamese like the ones you used to bring here."

"Aww, that's a sweet memory. The Siamese loved your house. Do you remember them chasing each other up the stairs?"

"More like flying."

"You bet, Grammy. I plan on at least two, so they can play together and keep each other warm at night."

Pearl laid the piece of paper she'd been reading on the bed. She reached over and took a glass of water off the bedside table. She took a sip, then asked, "Why didn't you tell me you were having problems with Ray?"

"I don't know. I guess because I didn't want you to think I was a failure."

"I love you, Emma. I'd never think that."

"I haven't told anyone, except you, of my plans. Grammy, for your safety and mine, if anyone asks about me, please lie and say you don't know where I am, what I'm doing."

"I won't have to I lie because you didn't tell me. If anyone asks, I don't have a clue where you are."

"Good. Let's keep it like that."

"Can I ever tell Lawrence?"

Emma shook her head. "No, not even Lawrence."

"My lips are sealed, but what are you not telling me about Ray?"

"Ray is a control-freak. He's a manipulative monster. He'd make fun of me in public. He criticized me all the time."

"He sounds awful."

"He told me that if I ever left him, he'd track me down and kill me."

Pearl gasped. "Kill you? Did you call the police?"

"Grammy, you don't call the police when you're living with a gangster."

Pearl's mouth dropped and she repeated the word. "Gangster," she said, shocked. "Maybe you should call the police now! Right now!"

Emma sighed. "It's not necessary. By this time tomorrow, I'll be as far from Ray as possible."

Pearl thought for a second, then asked, concerned, "Does Ray know where I live?"

"I never told him. He doesn't have a clue. He was never interested in my personal back story."

"What did you see in him?"

"He was very charming at first, but then I realized he was a jerk."

"How long were you two together?"

"Little over six months."

"Did he ever hit you? Hurt you?" Pearl pried.

Emma looked down at her hands and began wringing them. She didn't answer. She didn't want to tell her dying grandmother that once Ray had beaten her so badly, she'd ended up in the hospital. Or how she stupidly went back to him when he begged her to do so.

Pearl gave a sad look, then said, "Enough said. You're free of him now. I want you to promise you'll never risk coming back here—*ever*."

"I can't do that," Emma said. "I love you."

"Okay, we'll work on that part. Maybe we can rendezvous somewhere, when I'm better."

"Better? Grammy you have stage five cancer." A tear slid from her eye.

"Oh, what do those doctors know," Pearl said with hope. "Let's change the subject. You need to get rid of your cell phone so he can't hire someone to track you down."

"I'm already on it. I bought a burner phone."

"What's that, dear?"

"You pay for it in cash. No personal questions asked. No contract. When I've used up the minutes, I'll dump it and buy another one."

"Smart girl."

"I don't know about that, Grammy. I'm certainly not very smart when it comes to picking men."

"Emma, don't sell yourself short. You're getting out of a terrible situation and making a new life for yourself. I'm sure you'll meet the man of your dreams. He's out there. You just need to find him."

"Thank you for your vote of confidence." Emma reached over and took Pearl's hand. "Grammy, I'm not staying the night. I have to leave now."

"But, no, Lawrence will be back. We're having dinner together like old times. Please say you'll stay," Pearl pleaded.

"I'll call you in a few days."

"I hope to hear from you sooner than that. Send me an email."

"I deleted my email account."

"Is that wise?"

"I don't want Ray emailing me. When I get settled, I'll open another account and use a different user name."

"Good idea."

"I also took down my Facebook and Twitter accounts, the list goes on."

Pearl smiled. "Sounds like you've thought of everything. Oh, before you go, I have something for you." She reached over and opened the drawer of her bedside table. She extracted a bank card. "Take this." Pearl placed a debit card in Emma's hand. "The pin number is your birthdate."

"Thank you *so* much. I'm glad you used my full name. I've decided I'm going by my middle name when I move."

"Oh, that's sweet. You do know your mom and dad named you after my godmother, Rachael? She was a sweetheart."

"Yes, Grammy. I remember you telling me."

Pearl smiled at the memory, then said, "I closed out my other account and opened up a new one, so use this card instead. You stand to inherit a large sum of money, and with this debit card, the money will be there for you when you need it."

Emma suddenly realized the gravity of the situation, and how seriously ill her grandmother was. Tears began to fall from her eyes.

"Come here, honey," Pearl said. "Let Grammy wipe those tears away. I love you."

"I love you, too," Emma sobbed.

Emma embraced her grandmother, then left the room. Tears blinded her as she walked outside. By the time she walked six blocks to the public library, her tears had dried up. She entered the building, signed in to use the computer under a bogus name, and found one at the back of the main floor. She looked around. She was the only user. She inserted the flash drive. Within a few minutes, she knew what was on it, and it wasn't good news. With mixed emotions, ranging from denial to terror, she thought, *Oh, no . . . no . . . Ray, what are you involved in?* Then she contemplated the deadly consequences of knowing his secret. She weighed her options. She could get on the bus, head to the bank in Atlantic City, and return the flash drive where she'd found it. She could go home to Ray and take his abuse for not bailing him out of jail. She could give up her dream of starting a new life away from him. Her heart was pounding. She had to make a quick flee-or-stay decision.

Her inner voice warned, *if you're going back to that low life Ray, you'd better hurry up and do it. Atlantic City isn't a hop-skip away from Nyack. It'll take you time to get there. You'll want to go to the bank before they close.*

Emma worried. *What if I'm too late? What if Ray or one of his criminal cronies are waiting for me at the bank?*

After careful consideration, Emma knew what she had to do. She removed the flash drive from the USB port, slipped it into her purse, then walked outside. Using her burner phone, she called a local car service to take her to LaGuardia Airport. She had a plane to catch. She'd worry another time about what to do with the flash drive, but for now, she was flying off to escape, and begin a new life.

Chapter Four

Charity Gone Ugly

Monday

Katherine finished putting out snacks on the dining room table for the two other members of the Kendall Charitable Foundation Board. Previously, she'd shut the pocket doors and the door to the kitchen from pesky felines, two of whom were notorious thieves when it came to pickpocketing guests or sneaking in and stealing food, especially snacks. The cats stood behind the closed doors and voiced their displeasure — a chorus of loud shrieks and caterwauls. Siamese sisters Scout and Abra jiggled the doorknob and pawed the kitchen door.

"Cut it out!" Katherine scolded the noisy cats.

The doorbell sounded its crisp ring and the cats fled to the upstairs cat playroom, except for Iris, who was waking up from a nap *under* the dining room table. Katherine hadn't noticed her, because the table was covered with an oversized tablecloth that nearly touched the floor.

"Saved by the bell," Katherine muttered. She moved to open the door. Chief London and Margie Cokenberger stood outside.

"Well, kiddo, are you going to let us in?" Margie asked in a teasing voice. "It's so hot out here you could fry an egg on the sidewalk."

"My car thermometer says ninety degrees. Feels cool in here," the chief commented.

"Hi, Chief. Hi, Margie. Come in." Katherine smiled and directed them to the dining room.

The chief looked around. "Where's the cats?"

"When they heard the doorbell, they fled upstairs. They're probably going to nap in their cat room."

"You mean catnap," the chief joked.

Margie asked, "Katz, when I die and go to heaven, can I come back and be one of your cats? They have it made in the shade."

Katherine slid open the dining room's pocket door and the three walked inside. Katherine quickly closed the door to prevent a possible cat invasion later.

The chief removed his tasseled hat and placed it on a chair. "I'm off-duty, but I didn't have time to go home and change out of my work clothes."

"That's perfectly okay."

"I didn't either," Margie seconded. "I just came from the job site. I've been working hard on that reno on main street."

"You mean the old antique store?" Katherine asked. "When is the new owner moving in?"

Margie sat down and grabbed a handful of pretzels. "When *is* she moving in? Now that's a story," Margie said with exaggerated emphasis. "When she wired me the deposit, she said she'd be here at the end of the month, then lo and behold, she showed up yesterday. I was fit to be tied."

"Why?" Katherine asked, surprised. "I thought you'd be pleased to show off what you've done to the place."

"I'd love to, but it's not finished! The paint is barely dry on the walls. I called Stevie to drop what he was

44

doing and come over and finish the electrical, but he said Salina and he had plans in the city, and he'd start first thing today. And you won't believe this part of the story. She stayed overnight without a piece of furniture and no electricity."

"Why didn't she stay at the Erie Hotel? It's next door," Katherine asked.

"She said she didn't want to. Later, Cokey and I felt sorry for her, so we took her a box fan and our inflatable guest bed, sheets and pillows and stuff so she wouldn't have to sleep on the dusty floor."

"Aww, Margie, that was so sweet of you two," Katherine praised.

"She was tickled pink when we showed up."

The chief sat down and grabbed a pretzel and popped it in his mouth. "What kind of vehicle is she driving?" he asked.

Margie answered, "She doesn't own a car. She said she was going to buy one soon."

"If she doesn't have a car, how did she show up? Parachute? Teleportation?" the chief asked with a mischievous look in his eye.

"Or beamed in like Captain Kirk in a Star Trek movie," Margie said with a grin. "What can I say? She just appeared. I was working in the kitchen and she waltzed in. She seemed to come out of nowhere."

"Mysterious," Katherine added. "So, I take it the front door was unlocked."

"Yep. My bad."

"Did you ask her any questions about how she got here?" Katherine asked. "Just curious."

"Nope, I was so surprised to see her, I didn't ask."

The chief, referring to how nosy Margie was, commented, "You're slipping."

Margie rolled her eyes. "But I do know, she wasn't very happy about us not being finished."

"Gosh, what did she expect?" Katherine asked. "She came early."

"Oh, don't get me wrong. She's a very nice person. I meant to say she was disappointed and didn't get the message that the place wasn't finished," Margie explained. "It's been rather hard to communicate with her."

"How's that?" the chief asked.

"She calls and leaves instructions on a voice mail, then when I try to call her back, I get this robot telling me I punched in an invalid number."

The chief scratched his short beard. "How many times has this happened?"

"Ah, about three times. It's been hard for me to coordinate the work, let alone ask her a question if something unexpected comes up."

Katherine suggested, "Have you tried texting?"

"Same thing. I type in this big ole message, send it, and it pops back 'Not Delivered' in ugly red letters."

The chief crunched on another pretzel. "What's the gal's name?"

"Rachael Thomas."

"Got her address?"

Margie smirked. "404 Main Street, Erie, Indiana."

The chief joked, "Not her address here. Where does she come from?"

"I don't have a clue, but I do know she bought the property through an LLC, which means—"

Katherine finished, "An LLC doesn't have to divulge personal information about its members or their transactions. In other words, there wouldn't be a public record of Ms. Thomas's place of residence when she bought the property. Chief, I don't see why it's so important. We'll find out soon enough when we welcome her to our little town."

"True, but this has piqued my interest, that's all," the chief said. He took out a small notebook, wrote down Rachael's name, then slipped it in his side pocket. He adjusted his weight on the chair and said, "Okay, Katz, I think we got sidetracked here, let's bring this meeting to order."

"And whose fault is that?" Margie teased.

"Okay, let's get down to the charity of the month," Katherine said, glad to change the topic of discussion and get down to business. "Last month, Mrs. Owen got a new dishwasher—"

Margie interrupted, "That was dramatic."

"What? How was it dramatic?" Katherine asked.

The chief chuckled. "Let's just say that Mrs. Owen doesn't take kindly to charity."

"What happened?"

Margie explained. "Mrs. Owen is ninety-years-old and as feisty as the day she was born. When the appliance store guy tried to deliver it, she stood on her front porch with a shotgun pointed at him."

"What?" Katherine gasped. "You're kidding me."

"She said she'd been washing her own dishes for a very long time and she didn't need a dishwasher."

"Refresh my memory. How did her name get on our charity list?"

"She has a son, daughter-in-law, and four kids that live with her," Margie said. "That's a lot of people who generate lots of dishes. Seems Mrs. Owen has memory problems."

The chief added, "Which normally isn't a good thing, but in this case, because of her bad memory, she forgot to load the gun."

"What happened then?" Katherine asked.

The chief chuckled. "I intervened, took the shotgun, and called her son to come subdue his mother or I'd have to arrest her for attempted assault."

Katherine's eyes grew wide. "You'd arrest a ninety-year-old woman?"

The chief put his hands up in mock defense. "Well, yeah. She was disobeying the law."

Margie added, "We solved the problem by having the delivery guy bring the dishwasher to my garage, until the son could be home. Cokey caught up with him at the diner and set up a time when he could install it."

"Whoa! Close call," Katherine said.

The chief said, "You know what they say about random acts of kindness?"

"What's that, Chief?" Margie asked.

"My wife says that for every act of kindness you perform, one more brick gets added to your path to heaven."

"That's so sweet of Connie," Margie said.

The chief reached in his back pocket and pulled out a dog-eared laminated photo of his wife. "See," he said, turning the photo over, "Connie wrote the saying on the back. Whenever I get down in the dumps or just want to look at my wife's pretty face, I take this out of my pocket."

"That is *so* precious," Katherine complimented, studying the photo. She handed it back to the chief, who returned it to his pocket.

Iris grew bored sitting under the table. The floor was hard. The humans were loud. The Siamese wanted to escape the room, but with the doors closed, she was trapped until the humans let her out. She stood up, stretched, and slipped her brown-velvet paw inside Margie's bag, which was lying on the floor with its flap open. Not finding anything of interest, she padded over to the chief and explored his back pocket. With a quick hook of a claw, she snagged a dog-eared photo. She dragged it under the table, then returned to see what else she could find. She spotted the chief's hat sitting on a side chair. Sneaking over to the chair, she snatched the tassels in her jaws and quietly dragged the hat to join the photo beneath the table.

"Okay, let's move on," Katherine prompted. "It's my turn to come up with a name for this month's charity. I've learned from Lizzie Howe, at the rescue center, that a neighbor had a terrible car crash, and broke her leg. She has a caregiver to tend to her needs, but she needs someone to visit every day to take care of her two cats, which are quite old."

"Geezer cats," Margie commented.

"Yes, exactly. One is sixteen-years-old and the other is twenty."

"Wow," Margie said. "That's old for cats."

The chief said, "The only woman I know who was in a serious auto accident is Ruth Reynolds."

"Yes, that's her," Katherine answered.

"I knew her husband. My wife and I went to his funeral. I don't understand why their daughter can't take care of her mom and her cats?"

"She moved to Florida and has no intention of coming up to care for her mother," Katherine said.

Margie piped in, "Ruth needs someone to come in once a day and solely tend to the cats. Easy as pie."

"Yes, but I was thinking about hiring a cat sitter to come in twice a day."

"Sounds good," the chief agreed.

Katherine smiled. "All in favor of the charity of the month going to Ruth Reynolds say aye."

"Aye," the chief said.

"Aye," Margie stated, reaching down and fumbling for her bag.

"All righty then," the chief said, getting up from his chair. "Until next month, ladies," then looking around the room, "Where's my hat?"

Underneath the table, Iris yowled guiltily.

Katherine lifted up the tablecloth and peeked at the blue-eyed, brown-masked cat. "Miss Siam, what are you doing in here?" she asked, surprised.

Iris sat on top of the chief's hat. She'd adjusted her body for the most comfort, with her paws tucked beneath her. She slowly blinked an eye kiss.

"Get off of that," Katherine scolded.

Margie laughed, then helped herself to more pretzels.

The chief got down on his hands and knees and said to Iris, "You know it's against the law to steal the Chief of Police's headgear."

Iris yowled sweetly. She got up, ceremoniously kicked the hat with her back legs, and plopped down on the photo so the chief wouldn't see it.

The chief laughed. He picked up his hat and brushed off a few cat hairs, then grinned. "What's a few hairs." Holding the hat in his hand, he walked to the front door. Margie followed him. Iris waited until the humans had cleared the room, then she retrieved the dog-eared photo. She bit into one of the ratty corners, then bound to the living room where she stored it with her other loot, in the lining of a blue wingback chair.

Chapter Five

Monday Afternoon

Stevie Sanders parked his red Dodge Ram outside the Erie High School and looked around for his daughter, Salina. Earlier he'd texted and said he was running late. When he didn't see her standing outside waiting for him, in the now-vacant parking lot, he texted again. *"I'm here. Out front."* Salina was taking a summer class in journalism. She was a natural at asking the right questions.

Stevie, a former prison inmate and drug runner, hadn't committed a crime in years. When his ex-wife, Darlene, overdosed on drugs, he gained custody of his teenaged daughter. Now, he was happy being a father and proud that his business interests had grown into a successful venture. At this point in time, he was happier than he'd ever been, but unhappy in finding the right woman to share his life with. His biggest obstacle was his friend and neighbor, Katherine Cokenberger. There wasn't a woman in the world that could live up to her, and if there was, he was convinced he'd never meet her. *If only Katz wasn't married*, he thought. *If only Jake was out of the picture, but that's never going to happen,* he ventured, then snapped out of his reverie.

Salina rapped on the passenger side window. "Dad, open up. I'm melting. I'm melting," she said dramatically.

Stevie unlocked the door. "Hey, Baby Cake, sorry I'm late."

"Where were you?"

"The boss lady has me hustling to finish the electrical in this old building downtown. I forgot the time."

"It's okay," Salina said, getting in. "I was about to text KC to see if she could pick me up."

"Two peas in a pod," he joked. "You really like her, don't ya?"

"Ah, duh?" Salina teased.

Salina threw her bookbag on the floorboard and hopped up onto the passenger seat. "Dad, Shelly and I have been invited to a party. Can I go? Can I?" she asked excitedly.

"When is it?"

"This weekend."

"Where?"

"Julie Baxter's house."

"Who's Julie Baxter?" Stevie pressed.

"She's the most popular girl in school."

"Why have I never heard of her before?" he asked, pulling out of the school parking lot.

"Dad, what is this, the third-degree?"

"Is it a boy-girl party?"

"No, it's a girl party. A slumber party, Dad."

"I'll think about it," Stevie said, wanting to know more about this new friend whom Salina had never talked about.

"I know when you think about stuff, that means I won't be able to go," Salina pouted.

Stevie turned onto Lincoln Street and parked in front of their home, an American Foursquare.

"Home, sweet home," he said. "Why don't I fix a snack before dinner?"

Salina frowned, grabbed her bookbag, and climbed out of the truck. "Shelly's Mom and Dad are okay with it," she sassed, slamming the door. She stormed to the front door, then called back, "You never let me do anything."

Chapter Six

The Intruder

Rachael's Planned Café in Erie

Tuesday

Emma Rachael Thomas, now using her middle name, stood next to a tall bistro table in the first-floor storefront of her planned café. It was the only piece of furniture in the entire three-story building. She flipped open her laptop and did a Google search on what she needed to do to open a restaurant. First, she required a local business license to operate, a food-handler permit, and an employer ID number. Next, she had to obtain a sales tax permit from the state government. From all of this and the related tons of paperwork, she feared information about where she lived might become a public record. "Public record" meant Ray and his mob friends would find and kill her. Fortunately, she didn't put the cart in front of the horse. She hadn't ordered the expensive commercial kitchen appliances, because the more she explored the opening of a café, the more she thought it was becoming a very bad idea.

Rachael was happy that the remodeling of the upper two floors were finished, so she could shop for furniture. She was tired of sleeping on a borrowed inflatable mattress and longed for a normal bed.

The first floor was almost complete. The kitchen was finished except for the restaurant-grade appliances, sink, dishwasher, stove and refrigerator. The white cabinets and butcher block counters were installed. *If I don't pursue the café idea, I could have regular kitchen appliances installed. And when the electricity is hooked up, I'll be good to go*, she thought. *I have a feeling that will be soon.*

She glanced over at the electrician kneeling on the floor, installing new receptacle outlets. He was the reason why she was in the storefront, and not in the kitchen where she normally set up her laptop.

After her last devastating relationship, she couldn't believe she was attracted to another man, but he was so different from Ray. He had impeccable manners, he never used raunchy curse words, and he . . . he . . .. Rachael pinched herself and thought, *Danger! Proceed with extreme caution.* Then she stole another look at the electrician, who was screwing on a wall plate cover. She loved his deep, midwestern accent, his shyness around her, and the fact he was one of the handsomest men she'd ever seen: blond-haired with piercing blue eyes, tall and obviously in great physical shape.

Stevie Sanders, a man with a criminal past, noticed her glance and stood up. "Ma'am, you're making way too much noise. It's hard to concentrate." He then smiled.

Rachael returned a serious look, then realized he was kidding. She smiled back and played the game. "I haven't said a word. You're the one who's noisy."

Stevie held up his screw driver. "Not my fault. Blame it on Walter."

"Walter? Who's Walter?"

"My screw driver."

"Do you normally name your tools?"

"Sure, why not?"

A loud noise came from the kitchen. Something heavy crashed to the floor.

Rachael startled. Fear washed over her face. She quickly moved to the front of the storefront and crouched down in the corner.

Stevie caught her emotion. "Hey, look, it's okay. I'll check it out." He ran into the kitchen, holding his screw driver like a deadly weapon. In the kitchen, he found the back door open. He moved to close it, then he found several small cooking pots scattered on the floor. He saw the movement of a black kitten darting for cover under the opening for the new sink.

"Come here, you little rascal. I'm not going to hurt you," he said gently.

The kitten came out and made a beeline for Stevie. It hooked its little claws on Stevie's work pants and started to climb. Stevie reached down and lifted up the frisky kitten. He cradled it in his arms. "Ah, you're a cute little darlin'."

Heading out of the kitchen, he called, "Coast is clear. I found your intruder."

Rachael was shaking so hard, she couldn't answer. She didn't want Stevie to see how terrified she was, but she couldn't hide the fact that she was scared to death. She thought Ray had shown up to do what he said he was going to do to her — kill her, or beat her so badly she'd be in the hospital.

"Ma'am," Stevie called. He approached her and saw how disturbed she was. "It's okay. No need to fret. Your kitten pushed some pans over."

Rachael rose and said in a nervous voice, "I don't have a kitten."

"No?" Stevie asked, surprised.

"No," she said, taking the kitten from Stevie, and petting it. The kitten purred loudly.

"Well, if this isn't your kitten, I guess we need to find out who he or she belongs to."

Rachael lifted the kitten in the air and examined the feline. "It's a girl."

"My friend Katz can hook you up with someone at the Erie Rescue Center. We can take the kitten there." Stevie pulled out his cell phone.

"Oh, no, please don't call anyone. I've been meaning to get a cat."

Stevie shoved the phone back into his pocket. "As you wish, but with all the critters in this town running loose, you need to keep your door closed."

"Normally, I do, but this morning, I was out back in the patio area trying to tidy up that god-awful flower bed. I propped the kitchen door open to catch a breeze; it has been so hot with no air-conditioning. The kitten must have come in then."

"We better check outside to see if this kitten has a mama looking around for her missing baby."

Stevie walked to the back door; Rachael followed him, still holding the kitten. Stevie walked outside and searched the small, enclosed area, which consisted of a tall, brick wall and concrete patio bordered by a weed-choked, overgrown flower garden.

"Yeah, I see what you mean about god-awful flower bed. It looks like something you'd see in an abandoned cemetery," he chuckled.

Rachael laughed, then asked, "Do you see any more cats?"

"Nope." Stevie looked at the brick wall that adjoined the back area of the hotel. It was covered with matted vines. "I think your intruder scaled the vines on this connecting wall."

"Or came in through the gate. I had it open for a little while."

"I can go next door to see if they're missing a kitten?" Stevie suggested.

"Why would the hotel have a kitten?"

"The owners keep several cats out back in the loading dock area. The cats are supposed to be fixed."

"Why? That doesn't make any sense."

Stevie misinterpreted what she'd asked. "So, they don't have kittens."

"No, I mean, why do the owners have cats in the loading dock and not in the hotel?"

"The cats are barn cats."

"What's the difference?"

"Barn cats are good mousers."

"Oh," Rachael laughed. "I get it. Pest control. I guess I have a lot to learn here."

"You mean folks on the east coast don't have mousers?"

Rachael was taken aback by the question and asked nervously, "How did you know I was from the east coast?"

"Your accent is a dead giveaway. A New Yorker, right?"

"Sort of," Rachael said guardedly.

"Like I said, you have to meet Katz. She's from New York, too."

"We better get this baby inside," Rachael said, changing the subject. She headed for the back door. She waited for Stevie to go in first, then once inside, she shut the door and set the black kitten on the floor.

"Aww," Rachael said. "She's precious."

"She looks healthy." Stevie glanced around the kitchen, noting the missing sink. "Where do you get your water?"

"I buy bottled water."

"Then bust out some for this kitten. It's hard telling how long she's been outside. The little girl needs a drink."

Rachael took a bowl out of the cabinet and filled it with water. She set the bowl down on the floor. The kitten slurped the water with her tiny tongue.

They both watched the kitten drink for a long time.

"I think you should name her Intruder," Stevie said, running his hand through his hair.

Rachael reflected and thought about the name for a moment. She nodded. "Perfect. I like that." Then she said, "I'll have to take her to a vet for a check-up and her baby shots."

Stevie winked. "Sounds like a plan. How old do you think she is?"

Rachael picked up the kitten and looked inside her mouth. She counted the number of teeth, then looked at the cat's eye color, which was a deep amber. "I'd say she's almost four- or five-months-old."

"How can you tell?"

Rachael didn't answer right away. She didn't want to mention that she had some vet tech training, but had changed her major when she discovered she couldn't stand the sight of blood. She'd already screwed up by not denying to Stevie that she was from New York. "Oh, I really don't know," she said cautiously. "We'll see what the vet has to say."

"Mew," the kitten cried.

"If you're keeping her, you'll need to get some cat things."

"Cat things?"

"For starters, she'll need a litter box, litter, and food."

"I can make a temporary litterbox out of a small cardboard box. I can tear up some newspaper."

Stevie nodded, then headed back to the front of the storefront. He called back to Rachael in the kitchen, "I'll be finished in a few minutes, then I'll turn on the AC before we suffocate."

"Wonderful," she answered.

Stevie installed the last outlet, then screwed on the wall plate. He returned to the kitchen, found the breaker box in the utility closet, and turned on the main switch. Then he walked to the front of the building to the programmable thermostat and tapped it to select air-conditioning mode. Cool air began circulating throughout the building.

Rachael returned. She walked over and stood in front of the wall register. "Yay. Thank you so much."

"You're welcome, ma'am."

"Mr. Sanders, can I ask you a favor?"

"Yes, ma'am."

"My name is Rachael, not ma'am."

"My name is Stevie, not Mr. Sanders."

"Okay, Stevie."

"What's your favor?"

"I haven't had time to buy a car yet—"

Stevie cut her off. "I can drive you to the pet store."

"That's very kind of you, but I can call an Uber."

"Uber," Stevie repeated.

"Yes, you've heard of them, right?"

"Yeah, but not around these parts. Erie doesn't have a car service, taxi cab, or anyone signed up to drive for Uber or Lyft."

Rachael wrinkled her nose in an attractive way. "In that case, I'm looking to buy a pre-owned car."

"I can help you with that. I'll keep my eye out for a nice, used car. I'll even check it out for you."

"I would appreciate that very much, but until I get wheels, can I take you up on your offer to drive me to a pet store?"

"Yes, ma'am. I mean Rachael. I'm officially finished."

"Great. In the future, I'll order pet supplies online, but today I really need a bunch of supplies for this kitten."

"I take it you're keeping her."

"How'd you know?"

"Because your face just lit up like a Christmas tree."

Rachael grinned, then asked, "Oh, is there a restaurant close to the pet store? I want to treat you to dinner."

"Yes, there is, but—"

Rachael interrupted, "Oh, I'm sorry if you already have dinner plans. It was presumptuous of me to assume."

"It's okay. I wanted to ask you if my daughter could come along, too? I told her I'd cook dinner tonight, but I'd much rather go out."

"You have a daughter? Oh, wait, are you married? I didn't see a ring." Rachael stopped, realizing her faux pas. Every woman knows checking for a man's wedding ring is a sign of being interested.

Stevie smiled through the mistake, but didn't say anything.

Rachael continued, "I mean, oh gosh, I don't know what I meant. I'm not very good at this," she said, trying to find the right words to get out of an awkward situation.

"I'm not an expert on these matters, but I think you did a terrific job looking for a ring," Stevie teased. He held his left hand up to prove the point. "I'm single. I'm not seeing anyone. I have a teenaged daughter. Her mother, my ex, died several years ago."

"I'm sorry to hear that."

"My daughter's name is Salina. She's fifteen, and loves cats."

"She does?" Rachael asked happily, starting to relax. "This is perfect."

"In fact, when I go home to change out of my work clothes, I'll rustle up some food for the kitten. I'm sure Wolfy won't mind if we take a few cans of his favorite food."

"Wolfy?"

"My daughter's cat, Wolfy Joe. He's a big, old gray cat. Salina and I will bring the food back to you."

"You are very kind," Rachael said seriously. "Thank you."

"Oh, and Rachael, when I take two wonderful ladies out to dinner, it's my treat, got that?"

Rachael hesitated, then said, "Okay."

"No problem. Pick you up at six?" Stevie said, packing up his toolbox and leaving.

"Yes, that would be great," Rachael said, locking the door behind him. She leaned against the door and whispered, "Take it one step at a time. He's really nice, but Ray was nice, too, when I first met him."

Chapter Seven

Unexpected Reunion

Wednesday

Rachael drove her pre-owned Toyota Tercel in front of the pink mansion and parked. She climbed out of the car and walked up the steps to the front door. A heavy gust of wind nearly toppled her tiny frame. With one hand, she moved a long strand of hair from her face so she could see, and with the other, she grasped her Boho gypsy skirt so she could walk. A sudden clap of thunder made her jump. She hurried to ring the doorbell.

Katherine was in the atrium, picking up shards of glass, from what had once been a beautiful Nippon vase. It was her late great-aunt's and held special meaning, but not anymore. Yesterday, she'd moved the vase to a different table so she could dust. She'd forgotten to put the vase back in its safe spot. Sometime during the cats' morning steeplechase race, one of them had jumped up onto the table and knocked off the vase. She suspected the youngster Dewey. He wasn't exactly graceful when trying to win the race. She muttered ruefully, "Not one of my smarter cat-proofing moments."

The doorbell sounded loudly.

"I'm coming," Katherine said, moving to the door. She looked out the sidelight first and observed an attractive blond-haired woman in her thirties standing on her porch.

"Hello, may I help you?" she asked, still holding the dustpan in her hand.

A second round of thunder boomed overhead.

"Do I know you?" Katherine asked, not offering to open the door any further than a few inches. She'd learned from past experience to trust no one, especially since the pink mansion was a murder magnet.

"Oh, I'm sorry, my name is Rachael Thomas. I'm new to town. I bought the storefront next to the Erie Hotel. I heard so much about you that I thought I should stop by and introduce myself."

The wind grew in intensity and a heavy rain began to pour.

"Come in. Come in," Katherine invited, "Or we'll both be drenched." Katherine directed Rachael into the front parlor. She leaned the dustpan against a side table.

"Did I catch you at a bad time?" Rachael observed the pile of broken shards.

"One of my cats broke a vase. I was cleaning up the mess so they don't step in it and get a glass sliver in their paws."

"Ouch, that would hurt."

"Indeed, it would," she said, then paused, "By the way, I'm Katherine Cokenberger, but most people call me Katz."

"Pleased to meet you. Wow," Rachael said, looking around at the Victorian furnishings and the ornate fireplace surround. "This room is amazing. What am I saying? Your house is amazing, too. Have you lived here long?"

"I moved here in 2013. Please, take a seat," Katherine offered.

Rachael sat on an Eastlake parlor chair. She leaned over and placed her satchel purse underneath the chair, then arranged her long skirt for maximum comfort.

Katherine sat on the loveseat next to the fireplace. "Margie Cokenberger said she remodeled your building. Margie is the best. Last year, she remodeled my attic."

"Yes, she did an excellent job. I haven't really spoken to Margie much. We conducted a lot of business playing telephone tag. Is she a friend of yours?"

"Yes, we've been friends for several years now."

"The electrician has been very nice to me. He's amazing."

Katherine asked surprised, "Stevie Sanders?"

"Uh huh, Stevie."

"Stevie and his daughter live next door, in the Foursquare."

"Uh huh." Rachael nodded. "Salina is her name. I met her last night. He's very blessed to have her as his daughter."

Katherine wanted to ask the new gal in town more questions about Stevie, but instead asked, "I heard you're opening a new restaurant—"

"Café," Rachael corrected. "I want my café to be a warm, cozy place to sit and read a book, chat with friends, or hook up with new friends. Plus, there'll be an amazing selection of coffee, tea, cookies and muffins."

Katherine thought, *she uses that word amazing a lot*, then said, "Oh, like a coffee bar. I love that idea. I've missed my Brooklyn coffee bar since I moved here."

"Brooklyn? Where in Brooklyn?"

"Bay Ridge."

"Oh, I've been there. I went bar hopping with my friends. We found this great Irish pub. The band was incredible."

"When was that?"

"Oh, back in the day," Rachael answered evasively, then changed the topic. "Stevie said you were affiliated with the Erie Rescue Center."

"Well, yes and no. I have a Director, Lizzie Howe," Katherine answered, but didn't mention that her money paid and continued to pay for the no-kill shelter.

"I'd like to volunteer."

"That would be wonderful, but I thought you were opening a café. Won't that take up a lot of your time?"

Rachael shook her head. "I've run into some obstacles, so I've decided to not open it right away. I just moved to town, so I'd like to take things slow."

"Okay, that's great. I'll give you her number."

Rachael reached under her chair and drew out her purse. She unzipped it, grabbed a slip of paper and pen, then returned the purse back under the chair. "Yes, thanks, I need the address, too?"

"The main number is 762-3513. Ask for the volunteer coordinator, Nicholas. The Center is located south of town, a few miles out on Highway 41."

"Thanks, oh, also, can you recommend a vet? I have a new kitten who needs to be spayed."

Katherine gushed, "Aww, a baby. My vet is Dr. Sonny. His office is on the outskirts of town. Take the main street out of Erie, head north, and you'll see his clinic on the left."

Rachael finished writing down the information. She slipped the paper and pen in one of her side pockets. "Thanks for the info."

Katherine was poised to ask more questions about the kitten, but the doorbell rang. She rose from the loveseat. "One second. Hold that thought. I want to hear more about your new baby." She darted to the door and opened it.

Salina stood outside. "Hey, KC, can I play with the cats?"

"Sure. They'd love to see you. Come in."

Salina slipped off her raincoat. "Where should I put this?" she asked, holding up the dripping coat.

"Put it in that giant urn."

"Good place. Whose car is that?"

"It belongs to Rachael Thomas. She says you know her."

Salina gave a quizzical look. "Why is she here?"

"You can ask her. She's in the parlor."

Salina walked in and smiled at the guest. "Hey, Rachael."

"Hello, Salina."

"Wow, you really got a car fast."

"I took a walk this morning and found a used car place. I bought the Tercel. It's older, but that's okay. It runs."

"Did Dad help you find it?"

"No, he didn't, but I appreciated his offer of helping me find one. I'll have to let him know that I bought one."

"That's okay. I can tell him."

Katherine eyed Salina curiously, and wondered if Salina was a little bit jealous of the newcomer. She switched gears, "Rachael was just starting to talk about her new kitten."

Rachael answered proudly, "She's black with pointed-ears and a flat nose. I'm sure she's part Siamese because she's very vocal."

Katherine exclaimed, "Aww. How old do you think she is?"

"Probably about five months."

"Definitely weaned."

Salina jumped in. "Tell Katz what you named her."

"I named her Intruder, because that's what Stevie called her when the little girl invaded my house." Rachael laughed.

"Broke into your house? How did she get inside?"

"I left the kitchen door open to air out the place. Stevie and I were in the other room. Intruder walked in to my kitchen like she owned the place. She tipped over some pots and pans, and made such a noise, we thought someone had broken in."

"Where did she come from?"

"We don't know. Stevie said she might belong to the Erie Hotel so we carried Intruder next door and asked the owner. She said the kitten was cute but didn't belong to her."

"Finders, keepers, losers, weepers," Salina said, dropping her bookbag on the floor. She turned and asked Katherine, "Where are the cats?"

"I locked them in their playroom."

"Why?"

"Because they did a bad, bad thing."

Salina wrinkled her nose. "Broke something?"

Katherine nodded.

"Expensive?"

"Very."

"Have they served their sentence? Can I bust them out of jail?" Salina giggled.

"Yes, I think they've done their time."

Salina bounded upstairs.

Rachael commented, "Stevie said you had Siamese. I love Siamese. They are my most favorite breed. Very smart and always up to something."

"My husband, Jake, and I have six Siamese. Five seal-points and a lilac-point. Plus, a ruddy-ticked Abyssinian."

A herd of rambunctious felines darted into the room. In three fluid leaps, Lilac, Abby and Crowie used the back of the loveseat as a springboard and vaulted to the parlor picture-window valance.

"That was quite a jump," Rachael praised the cats.

While everyone focused their attention on the leap of the century, Iris crouched down with her belly skirting the floor and slowly crept under Rachael's chair. The Siamese began pawing inside Rachael's purse. It was the perfect set-up for the sneaky feline because Rachael's long, flowing skirt obstructed the humans' view. Iris quickly found her prize, clamped down on it, and quietly made her way to the next room where she stashed her stolen loot.

Scout and Abra hung back and stood at rapt attention, staring at the newcomer. Their sapphire-blue eyes grew big and their ears swiveled forward and backward in surprise.

Rachael turned her gaze to Scout and Abra. Her mouth dropped. "No, it can't be," she whispered, wide-eyed with shock.

Salina, now sitting on the floor, yanked her phone out of her schoolbag and began shooting video of Rachael.

"What?" Katherine asked, turning to look at the Siamese.

Rachael leaned forward in her chair. "Abra? Cadabra?" she called. "Come here."

Katherine was speechless, and for a moment didn't know what was going on.

"Is it you?" Rachael continued, to the Siamese.

"Ma-waugh," Scout cried. "Raw," Abra seconded.

The Siamese ran for Rachael and hopped on her lap. They reared up and head-butted her chin. Rachael wrapped her arms around them and buried her face in their fur. She started to cry. "Oh, my. Oh, my. I can't believe this. I'm so happy you're together."

Salina continued filming, and stopped when Scout and Abra jumped down.

The Siamese leaned on Rachael's legs.

"Do you need a tissue?" Katherine asked.

"No, I'm okay. It's just that," she choked, "I never thought I'd see them again."

"Scout? Abra? Are you okay?" Katherine asked, still in shock from what had just happened.

Abra trotted to Katherine and reached up to be held. Katherine picked her up and cradled her in her arms. Abra quivered against her. "It's okay, little one," then to Rachael, "How do you know them?"

Rachael ignored the question, then asked, "Scout? Is that what you call Cadabra?"

"I haven't called Scout that name for a long time. She doesn't like it."

Abby soared down from the valance, onto the back of the loveseat, to the floor. She bounded out of the room and joined Iris in the next room.

Rachael abruptly got up, reached under her chair and grabbed her purse. "I need to go," she said, heading for the door.

Katherine followed her. "Are you going to be all right?" she asked.

"Yes, thank you so much for your concern, but I'm fine. I just realized I'm late for an appointment. I'll show myself out."

Rachael hurried to the door, opened it, and rushed out, running to her car to get out of the rain.

Salina walked in and stood next to Katherine. "Wow, that was weird."

Katherine nodded. "Very weird."

"Hey, get back," Katherine said to Iris, who had shot out of the living room and was trying to get outside. "What's the matter with you?" she scolded the rowdy cat. Katherine quickly closed the door.

Salina asked, "How does she know Scout and Abra? Why did she call Scout a different name?"

"Believe it or not, I have a strong feeling that Rachael had something to do with the Hocus Pocus show."

"The what?"

"Harry DeSutter. The magician. Scout and Abra were in one of his acts."

"Oh, yeah, I remember you telling me about it."

"I suspect that Rachael worked for the magician in some capacity, like an animal trainer or handler."

Salina snickered, "A Siamese cat wrangler."

"Something like that."

"It was strange," Salina said. "One second she's happy to see them, then the next she's running out of the house like it's on fire."

"I agree."

Salina walked back to the parlor and extracted her schoolbag. "Got to go, KC."

"What's your hurry?"

"I need to go home and feed Wolfy Joe."

"Okay, talk to you soon. Oh, don't forget your raincoat."

"Yep, got it." Salina put on the coat, left and headed to her house next door. On the front porch, and out of the rain, she stopped and texted her friend, Shelly. With thumbs flying, she typed, "*I have an amazing video to post on YouTube. Can you come over and help me edit it? It's way too long and I don't know how to delete stuff.*"

Three seconds later, Salina's phone pinged. "*It's raining,*" Shelly texted with a sad face emoticon.

"*Please, please with sugar on top,*" Salina begged.

"*Oh, all right. I'll be there in a sec.*"

"*Cool,*" Salina texted.

A few minutes later, Shelly, carrying a wide umbrella, walked as fast as she could to Salina's house, two blocks away. She pounded up the front steps and rang the bell. Salina was waiting for her. She held Wolfy Joe, who was wriggling to get down.

Shelly petted his head.

"Hang on while I put him in the kitchen. I'll lock him up so he can eat and not bug us."

Salina left with the hungry cat, then returned.

"What's the dealy-o?" Shelly asked.

"When I was at KC's, this woman who my dad likes—"

Shelly interrupted, like she'd just heard a juicy bit of gossip, "Your dad has a girlfriend?"

"He calls her a lady-friend," Salina answered. "Any who, I didn't call you over here to talk about my dad. I need you to help me edit this video and get it online."

"Oh, yeah. The video. Is it on your phone?"

"Yeah."

"We have to copy it onto your hard drive. Let's go to your computer and do that. After that's done, I'll show you how to edit it."

"You're such a computer whiz," Salina teased.

"So, what do you want edited?"

"I want to delete a part of it, to make it shorter."

"Can do."

"I also want to add a short narrative."

"Can do that, too, but first, spill the beans. What's the big deal?"

"Dad's lady friend was visiting KC."

"Duh! I understand that part."

"I went over to play with the cats. KC had locked them in their playroom because one of them had broken something. When I went upstairs to see them, I let them out. They ran downstairs and barged into the room KC and Rachael were in."

"That's what you filmed? Why would anyone want to watch that online?" Shelly questioned with a serious look.

"Because the Siamese recognized Rachael."

"How could the cats know her?"

"Not all the cats. Just Scout and Abra."

"Okay, move on. I can't stay long. Mom wrote out a list of chores for me to do before she gets home from work."

"KC thinks Rachael was the cat wrangler to the magician. She took care of Scout and Abra."

"You mean that guy who mistreated Abra?"

"Yeah, that one."

"No way! That was like a hundred years ago. How would Scout and Abra remember her? And what's she doing in Erie if she's a famous cat wrangler?"

Salina shook her head. "I don't know, but it's such a cool story, I have to post it online. I wish you could have been there. It was such a sweet reunion."

"I see your point, but we'll have to come up with a catchy title. How about "*Woman reunites with cats she hasn't seen in years*?" Shelly proposed.

"Not bad, but I think we should mention the woman's name or what her connection was to the cats. I mean, in the summer class I'm taking, my teacher said that a good journalist must write the five W's."

"Five W's?"

"Who, what, when, where and why," Salina answered.

"But isn't that a lot of information for one title?"

Salina thought for a moment, then suggested, "How about *Rachael Thomas reunites with Siamese cats*?"

"Okay, but we need to tell the viewer what Rachael's job was. How did she know the cats? Was she an animal trainer? Did she jump out of a hat?" Shelly launched into a fit of giggles.

"Did she get sawed in half in a box?"

"Google the magician's name and see what pops up."

Salina did the Google search on Harry DeSutter.

They both read the results on the monitor.

"There's not a single word about a cat wrangler. Press on one of those links," Shelly said.

Salina clicked on the link. An article from 2009 appeared from a newspaper, which reported the theft of a valuable stage performer named Abra.

"Eureka. Read more."

"Emma Thomas, a professional cat wrangler, is the prime suspect."

The girls stopped reading and exchanged curious glances.

Salina said, "Emma Thomas, not Rachael Thomas?"

"Maybe the reporter got the name wrong."

"A good journalist wouldn't do that."

"Maybe they were sisters who both worked for the magician?"

Salina shook her head. "That doesn't make any sense."

"Ok, so when your dad gets home, ask him to find out if Rachael was a cat wrangler."

"Why?"

"So, we can put her name in the title."

"I'll ask him, but in the meantime, I want to put the video online. Why don't I title it, *"Former cat wrangler reunites with Siamese cats she hasn't seen in years?"*

"Too many words, but not bad. We'll tweak it a little."

Chapter Eight

Later that Evening

Katherine sat on the wood atrium floor. Scout and Abra were cuddled on her lap. The other cats had fled upstairs when they heard the first clap of thunder.

Jake walked in from the back of the house. "Weather channel says another storm's heading our way."

"I think it's already here."

"You don't look very comfortable sitting there," he observed.

"I'm not," Katherine answered. "My leg's been asleep for an hour," she exaggerated. "When I try to get up, they both throw a cat fit."

"Let me take over," he said, sitting down next to her. He moved both Siamese and held them close.

Katherine stood up and sat down on the settee, "Thanks."

"What's going on with you two? Why are you being so clingy?" he asked the cats.

"Ever since Rachael Thomas was here, the girls have been restless."

"Maybe Rachael's presence conjured up bad memories for the Siamese?"

"I don't think their memories are entirely bad or else they wouldn't have jumped on her lap."

"True."

"I have a hunch she had something to do with the Hocus Pocus show."

Abra hissed; Scout growled.

"Girls. Girls. It's okay," he comforted. "You're safe with us. Katz and I would never let anyone harm you."

"They really get upset when we mention anything to do with that show."

Jake noted, "I'd say Rachael was an animal handler."

"I think so to. She gave it away when she called the cats by their showbiz names, and miraculously the Siamese went right to her."

"I'll have to try that the next time I want them to do something for me," Jake joked. "Usually, they do the opposite of what I want."

"She definitely cared for them in some capacity. I'd say she was a cat wrangler."

Jake sighed. "I'd love to get past this part of Scout's and Abra's history."

"I thought we had, but with Rachael showing up today, her visit puts us right back into the vicious circle."

"Katz, it was pure coincidence she had a connection to the girls."

"I'm not sure I believe in coincidences. I'm suspicious that she moved to Erie to —"

Jake read her mind and finished, "To take them. Nah, I don't think so. Random events like this happen all the time. It's a part of life."

Katherine shook her head. "I'm not convinced."

Scout and Abra grew tired of Jake's attention, rose and trotted over to Katherine. They collapsed against her legs, for one blissful moment, then began to wrestle. Abra bit Scout on the neck. Scout returned the favor. The two launched off of Katherine's legs and scampered up the stairs.

"Ouch," Katherine complained, rubbing her leg.

"Whoosh," Jake said, amused. "I guess their feline funk is over."

Katherine smiled.

Jake got up. "Come to the kitchen. If you toss the salad, I'll bake a couple of salmon steaks."

At the mention of fish, Scout and Abra began shrieking at the top of the stairs, in their "*I'm excited about getting salmon tidbits*" voice.

A flash of humor crossed Jake's face. "Hurry up and run before seven cats charge down here. Last one to the kitchen is a rotten egg."

Katherine raced ahead of him.

"Cheater," he called after her.

Chapter Nine

A Bar in Atlantic City

Thursday

Marcel Blumberg, a man in his late sixties, with silver-gray hair, was dressed in a designer business suit. He sat at the bar drinking a vodka martini. He scanned the room for Ray Russo, who was supposed to meet him an hour ago.

Marcel worked for one of the top casinos in Atlantic City, but quit when he decided his legitimate job was not paying for his lifestyle of collecting expensive houses, cars, and women. He also decided that illegal loans to compulsive gamblers wasn't generating the income he wanted either, but the new world of online banking was right up his alley. Internet money laundering was the name of the game, and where the big bucks were. He was riding high on the hog until Ray's mealy-mouthed fiancée, Emma, stole the flash drive that had the ledger on it. Since then, Marcel had to keep squeaky-clean, for fear that some big-shot authority would shut down his website. Or worse yet, the Feds would indict him for not registering his business with the Treasury Department.

Marcel blamed Ray for the foul-up. Ray was too lenient with that skinny broad. He should have corrected her when she did wrong. Better yet, he should have dumped her.

Marcel didn't get it. Ray was a handsome man. What did he see in her in the first place? She was a middle-class bookkeeper who worked nine-to-five, probably made zip in salary. She had dishwater-blonde hair, long and stringy, and she dressed like a throwback to the 1970s. But the biggest thing, besides Ray's bad taste in women, was how he set up a joint bank account with a woman he wasn't even married to, and shared a safe deposit box with her. All it took to mess up a good thing was for Emma to get ticked off at Ray, go to the bank and take the flash drive — the flash drive that had the account numbers and credentials for overseas accounts of every Tom, Dick and Harry. And the most incriminating contents were in-depth PDF files about the website, how it worked, who was involved, names of shell companies— enough information that could put a lot of people, including himself, behind bars for a very long time.

Marcel sighed. He wished he hadn't let the mob in on his cash cow. Now *they* were making demands for the return of the flash drive.

The mob boss wasn't pleased with Ray either. The word on the street was they would continue to protect Ray, but only if he found Emma and got the flash drive back. Also, those involved knew Emma could have made copies of the files, and if she did turn up, who could trust her to give up everything she had? *Hell, she could have handed over the flash drive to the FBI for all we know*, Marcel thought. That's why everyone in the business was minding their P's and Q's and worried that at any moment the bomb would drop on their operations.

Marcel knew Ray was doing everything he could to find Emma, which meant a huge outlay of cash — mob money — for private detectives and computer geeks to apply their online search skills. After a month, with no leads or information about Emma's whereabouts, people on the inside thought Emma had met her demise, but in truth, Emma had simply disappeared without a trace.

Ray walked into the bar and sat down next to Marcel. "Sorry I'm late," he apologized. "My new security job at the casino doesn't exactly have fixed hours."

"I don't know why you bother to work, when our business is raking in the dough."

"What can I say? I like working at the casino."

"Whatever," Marcel tsked dismissively. "I've been sitting here forever. You could have at least called."

"I don't make personal calls while I'm on the job, especially when I'm patrolling the casino floor."

"Relax. Order a drink."

"I don't mind if I do," Ray answered, then said to the bartender, "Bring me what Marcel's drinking."

The bartender went to the other end of the bar to mix the drink, then brought it back and set it down.

"Thanks," Ray said.

"No problem," the bartender said, moving to the middle of the bar to help another customer.

"Did you hear the news today?" Marcel asked.

"Enlighten me? Where's this going?"

"Remember Rose Martinez who was a co-worker of Emma's?"

"Yeah, I roughed her up, searched her phone and didn't find anything. What about her?"

"Her body washed up on the beach."

"What?" Ray asked, surprised.

"She's dead."

"When was this?"

"This morning." Marcel cast a suspicious look at Ray.

"Don't look at me. I didn't kill her," Ray answered in a low voice.

"It sounds fishy that she's dead. Maybe she knew more information about Emma than she told you. Maybe the boss had her bumped off?"

"Or she went out for a swim and drowned."

"On a work day?" Marcel asked incredulously.

"I'm not a psychic. The old biddy said she didn't know where Emma was, so I let her go. End of story. Did you kill her?"

"Fat chance," Marcel huffed. "I don't like to get my hands dirty. I'm just saying that it would be a shame that poor woman died for keeping Emma's whereabouts secret. According to the news, she had a big family and lots of grandchildren."

"Who cares! She's a dowdy old bag."

"She *was* a dowdy old bag. Now, she's in the morgue."

Marcel turned his attention to the TV monitor up high on the wall. The eleven o'clock news broke for a commercial. He slammed his fist on the bar. "Do you freakin' believe this? Another damn commercial."

"Take it easy! What's eating you?" Ray asked.

"I'm going to be drunk by the time they get to the sports segment."

"Maybe you should slow down on the drinking so you don't miss it."

"Right," Marcel said irritably.

The news came back on. The attractive female news anchor said, "We have lots of sports to talk about, but first let's show what's trending on social media. Posted on YouTube by *wolfy is fat* from Erie, Indiana. Attention cat lovers, you're going to love this."

A still image of Emma holding Scout and Abra was frozen on the screen.

The anchor continued, "Who says cats don't remember? This pair of Siamese cats haven't seen this woman in ten years, but look at their faces when they see her for the first time. Talk about a heartfelt reunion."

Ray wasn't paying any attention until he heard the anchor say something about a woman reuniting with

Siamese. He remembered Emma was always talking about these two Siamese cats she'd trained or took care of; he couldn't remember which. He leaned forward and stared at the screen. The video unfroze and started to play. On the screen, his missing fiancée sat in a chair with two cats on her lap.

Ray's mouth dropped open in astonishment.

The anchor announced in a perky voice, "In 2009, Emma Thomas worked for a magician who performed in the Catskills. After a performance, she was assaulted while taking care of the cats, which just finished their act. When she regained consciousness, one of the cats was missing."

Ray shouted at the barkeeper, "Hey, turn that up."

The bartender didn't answer but grabbed a remote and turned up the volume. He gave Ray a dirty look, then moved down to the other end of the bar.

The anchor said, "What a coincidence!"

Ray slid off of his barstool and continued staring at the screen.

Marcel choked on his drink. "Isn't that Emma?"

"Speak of the devil. The thief finally turns up."

Marcel started to say something else, but Ray put up his hand and shushed him.

After the short clip was over, the anchor finished, "What are the odds of that? From showbiz to a little town in Indiana called Erie."

Her voice droned on, but Ray wasn't listening. His face changed from one of shock to rage. "Erie, Indiana. I don't know where the hell that is, but I'm soon to find out," he spat.

"What are you going to do?"

"I'm going to track her down and get back what she stole from us."

"Why you? The boss might want to send somebody else."

"I don't want her dead."

"Then what are *you* going to do to her?"

"I'm going to make her so sorry she'll wish she hadn't been born," he threatened.

"Better tell the boss."

"I'm on it." Ray picked up his phone and stepped away from the bar to make the call. After a few moments, he returned. His face was red with anger.

"What did he say?" Marcel asked.

"He's sending somebody else because he doesn't want me to mess it up."

"What did he mean by mess it up?"

"How the hell would I know?"

Chapter Ten

YouTube Nightmare

Friday

Salina was ecstatic that her YouTube video had gone viral. She couldn't wait for her dad to get home so she could tell him. He was running late, which wasn't unusual, but then he pulled up in front, parked and walked to the house. Salina threw open the door, "Dad! Dad! I have to show you something."

"What?" he asked, taken aback by his daughter's excitement.

"Remember that video Shelly helped me edit, well, we put it on YouTube and it's gone viral."

"What video?"

"I told you about it."

Stevie shook his head. "No, you didn't. What's viral mean?"

"Everyone in the whole world is watching it!"

"That might be stretching it a bit," Stevie said with a gleam in his eye, proud of his daughter who was learning new computer skills every day. "Why don't you show it to me?"

"Come to my computer." Salina led the way to the back room where her computer was set up. "Hang on a minute, while I bring it up."

Stevie made himself comfortable in the chair next to her desk and waited patiently for Salina to play the video.

"Here it is! I took it the other day when Rachael visited KC. Watch it!"

Stevie's face clouded with worry. "Wait, you took a video of Rachael? Why would you do that?"

"Just watch it." Salina clicked the title and the video played.

Stevie said, concerned, "Rachael seems very upset. Does she know you did this?"

"Oh, I haven't shown it to her yet. I don't know her email address. Do you have it? I can send the link right now."

"Salina," Stevie began seriously. "You don't post videos of people without their permission."

Salina stuck out her lower lip and pouted. "Oh, you always find fault with me."

"Salina, you owe Rachael an apology. To make things right, I want you to apologize now. Get your stuff, then get in the truck," he said angrily.

Salina studied his face and realized he wasn't kidding.

Stevie left the house and got in his truck. Salina reluctantly followed him and climbed in. She sulked the entire way to Rachael's.

Stevie drove up to the storefront and parked behind Rachael's vehicle. He rang the bell several times. Salina brooded behind him.

Rachael finally answered the door and when she saw who it was, she smiled brightly. "Hello, you two."

"Howdy, Miss Rachael," Stevie said, "Can we come in for a minute?"

"By all means. Please do." Rachael opened the door wide.

Stevie and Salina strode in.

Rachael noticed Salina wasn't her usual bubbly self. "Everything okay?" she asked her.

Salina didn't answer. She cast her eyes down to the floor.

Stevie said in a *"get down to business"* voice, "Salina has something to show you."

"What do you have to show me?"

Salina began to speak in a shy, quiet voice, "I posted something on YouTube and it went viral."

"Why that's great, Salina. What did you post?"

"I can show you." Salina reached for her phone.

Stevie corrected, "It's better to see it on a bigger screen."

"I can't wait to see it. Follow me to the kitchen." Rachael led the way. She moved to her laptop and clicked on the YouTube icon. "What's the title I'm looking for?"

"Former Cat Wrangler Reunites with Siamese Cats."

Rachael looked up, worried.

Stevie caught the look. "I'm not one to beat around the bush, but my daughter filmed you the other day. She failed to get your permission."

Rachael entered the text description in the search window and the video appeared. Before she pressed the play arrow, she scanned down the main page and noticed that there had been millions of hits. Then she played the video, which included a short narrative Salina had dubbed in. She brought her hand up to her face, and began shaking her head. "Oh, no. Oh, no. Salina, what have you done?"

Salina was surprised and said innocently, "I thought you had a sweet reunion with Scout and Abra."

"I'm afraid you did more than that," Rachael answered but didn't elaborate. She had a terrible premonition that her cover had been blown, that Ray would see the video, and come after her, but then she relaxed a little. She knew that Ray wasn't one for surfing the Internet. "Salina, I'm going to log off. Do you remember your YouTube password?"

"Yeah, it's *wolfyjoe15*. Why?"

"Because you're going to log in and delete the video."

Salina nervously twisted a strand of hair. "But why should I delete the video when its already been shown on the news."

"News? What news?" Rachael blurted.

"National news."

Rachael brought her hand to her forehead and brushed her hair out of her face.

Stevie walked over and ran his hand through the back of her hair. "Hey, are you okay?" he asked tenderly.

"Not really. I think I need to go lie down. I've suddenly got a horrible headache."

Salina apologized, "I'm so . . . so . . . sorry. I shouldn't have done it without asking you. I'll delete it. Right now."

Rachael shifted from the counter-height stool and let Salina sit down in her place.

Salina keyed in a few keystrokes and deleted the video.

Rachael didn't speak but had a frown on her face.

Stevie understood the expression and said, "We're going now. I'm taking Salina home and then, I'll be back."

"Oh, that won't be necessary," Rachael said.

"It will," Stevie countered.

He took Salina by the arm and led her back to the truck. "I'm going to drop you off at the house, then I'm going back."

"But, Dad, I don't think she wants to see you. She said she had a headache."

"I just want to talk to her for a minute."

"Talk to her about what?"

"For starters, I'm going to make sure she doesn't sue us for invasion of privacy."

"Sue us. Why?"

"Because you didn't ask her permission before you posted your video. You gave personal details in your narrative."

"Dad, she won't sue us."

"How do you know that?"

"She likes you."

Stevie glared at his daughter. "How do you know that?" he asked again.

"Because she seems so happy around you."

"Is that a fact," he said, not convinced.

Changing the subject, Salina asked, "What am I supposed to do about dinner? It's your turn."

"Grill yourself a cheese sandwich, and by all means, do *not* post anymore videos on YouTube or anywhere else."

"I won't," she said under-her-breath.

"I mean it," he said firmly.

"Okay! Okay! I promise!"

"I might be late, so go to bed at your regular time."

"I will, but Dad, can I go?" Salina asked in a pleading voice.

Stevie misinterpreted the question. "Why? We just left there."

"No, Dad. I need your approval so I can go to Julie's party. She needs to know."

Stevie said angrily, "Absolutely not."

"But, Dad, please. I promise I won't do it again."

"You're not going. No ifs, ands, or buts."

Salina burst into tears.

Stevie didn't try to console her.

After they got back to the house, Salina ran to her room and slammed the door. Stevie went to his bedroom and changed out of his work clothes. He put on a summer t-shirt and a faded pair of jeans. Lacing up his sneakers, he made a quick call. "This is Stevie Sanders. Are you open?" he asked.

"Yep."

"Good. What ya got cookin' tonight?"

"BBQ."

"How late you stayin' open?"

"Till ten. Now why don't you stop flappin' your jaws and get on over here?" the owner asked. "Can't you see I've got hungry mouths to feed?"

"Will do," Stevie said, hanging up. He chuckled at the owner's abruptness. The owner, Chester, was a no-nonsense sort of guy.

Outside, he backed his service van to the front of the garage, and unlocked his Dodge Ram. He loaded up a couple of lawn chairs and a can of insect repellent.

When he parked in front of the storefront, Rachael's Tercel was gone. "Damn," he said, frustrated. "Where did she go?"

He didn't have long to wait because she returned shortly. He sat in his truck and waited for her to get out of the car. She was carrying a fountain drink in a Styrofoam container.

Stevie climbed out and approached her. "Still got that headache?" he asked.

"No, not really. I think I was having caffeine withdrawal."

"Have you had dinner?"

"Not yet."

"Good, me either. Why don't I carry you out for the best barbecue you've ever had?"

Rachael looked up at his handsome face. She started to say no, that she had other plans.

"You'll really be doing this ole boy a favor. I haven't eaten since breakfast. I'm starving," he said. "I bet you are, too?"

She hesitated. "Well, I don't know."

"Let me put it this way," Stevie said. His blue eyes twinkled. "I appealed to the higher power and arranged to have your schedule cleared."

"I don't have a schedule. Remember, I don't have a job?"

"I also cleared your social calendar as well."

"How did you manage that?"

"Intruder told me she'd take care of it."

"My kitten talks?" she asked, amused. "When did she tell you?"

"Earlier."

"She couldn't have."

"Why?"

"She's at the vet being spayed."

"Oh, she told me a few days ago."

"Yeah, right."

A car passed by, creeping along at a slow speed. Inside, the male driver watched out the window. Stevie waved at him. Then the driver sped off.

"Is that someone you know?" she asked, not looking at the driver's face.

"No, just being friendly. Now, how about that barbecue?"

Rachael laughed. "You don't take no for an answer. Which chariot are we taking?"

"My truck."

She headed to the truck's passenger side. Stevie opened her door.

"How do I get up in this thing?"

He pointed, "Step up on this bar and haul yourself in by pulling on this."

"Okay," she said, doing exactly what he said.

Stevie moved to the other side, hopped in and fired up the engine.

"Can you turn up the air? It's hot in here."

"Yes, ma'am," he said, fiddling with the controls. He drove several miles out of town, then turned onto a pot-holed road.

Rachael asked, "Where are we going?"

"I thought we'd go on a little drive in the country."

"Is the barbecue place in the country?"

"Yes, it is. In fact, it's across the road from my place."

"You have a second home?"

"No, I meant to say, that Chester's kiosk is across the road from the land I own. I inherited property from my late father."

"I'm sorry for your loss."

"I'm not," he muttered.

"How long ago did he pass away?"

"A few years ago."

"Cancer? Heart attack? Old age?" she quizzed.

"He was shot."

Rachael gasped. "What? Shot? Who shot him?"

Stevie grabbed his sunglasses from the center console and put them on. "Let me explain it this way. Katz Cokenberger has a best friend named Colleen. She's married to a Deputy Sheriff named Daryl. Daryl shot my dad, who'd pulled a gun on him."

Rachael scrunched her nose up in disbelief of what she'd just heard. "Was your dad innocent?"

"Never," he snickered. "My dad was the biggest criminal in these parts."

"He was? What kind of crime?"

"Meth labs, whore houses, other kind of drugs."

Rachael turned in her seat to study Stevie, then asked, "Are you a criminal, too?"

"Nope. I was, but I'm not now."

Stevie came to Chester's ramshackle kiosk, which during the winter months was known as the Snow Angel Farm, and also known for Chester's decadently delicious hot cocoa. In the summer, Chester served mouth-watering barbecue and heavily sweetened iced tea.

"It's really crowded. I might not find a parking space," Stevie observed. "Oh, here's one," he said, pulling in.

Rachael wasn't paying any attention to Stevie or to Chester's weather-beaten kiosk. Instead, she was busy looking out the window at a number of wind turbines. "Oh, wow, I heard Indiana had wind turbines."

"Yes, I'll explain after I get the grub." Stevie cut off his engine and got out.

"Should I get out?"

"Normally, I'd say yes, but people around these parts don't care for me much. There's an ugly rumor going around town about me and Katz."

"Katz? The woman in the pink Victorian?"

"I'll explain that, also. Now, what kind of sauce do you want on your sandwich? Mild? Hot? Flaming hot?"

"Mild," Rachael answered. "And fries."

"Chester doesn't make fries. How about chips?"

"Yes, thank you."

"Want more to drink?"

"I'm good."

While Stevie was standing in a queue to order the barbecue, Rachael yanked her burner phone out of her purse and called the veterinarian's office. The office was closed, but the night cleaning staff was there. She talked to a woman named Eva. She explained, "My kitten, Intruder, was spayed today. Could you check her cage and see how she's doing?"

"Ma'am, I'm not allowed to do that."

"Please. I'm a worried cat mom. Can you please go look? I won't tell anyone."

"Well, okay." There was a pause while the woman checked, then she returned to the phone. "She's okay. She's curled up in a little ball. Cutest thing I've ever seen."

"Thank you so, so much."

"You're welcome."

Rachael hung up and looked at Stevie, now first in line and ordering the food. She thought, *He's the nicest man I've ever met. Should I spoil the evening by telling him I have to leave? That, by this time tomorrow, Intruder and I will be miles from Erie.*

Stevie returned to the truck, carrying two bags. He handed the bags to Rachael. "Keep 'em warm," he teased.

"It's really hot outside. I don't think we have to worry about the food getting cold."

Stevie drove out of Chester's lot and pulled across the road. He drove several feet onto a paved lane and stopped. He pointed, "See those wind turbines?"

"Yes, I noticed them when we first got here. I find it surreal, in a kind of good way."

"Do you know why they're so tall?"

"No. Why?"

"Because the higher up they are, the windier it is. More wind equals more electricity."

"They are gigantic. I never knew they were so big."

"You're looking at about two hundred tons of steel."

"Amazing."

"I own the land that the wind turbines sit on."

"Okay, but who owns the wind turbines?"

"A big energy-conglomerate. They lease my land."

"How does it work?" she asked curiously.

"For every wind turbine you see out there, I get paid rent."

"Rent for each one?"

"Yes, each turbine."

"Excuse me for being nosy, but can you make a decent living off of—"

Stevie finished, "I earn a good living."

"How much?"

"I get paid about eight thousand per turbine."

"Per month?" she gasped at the figure.

"No, per year."

Rachael counted twenty turbines. *Twenty times eight thousand dollars equals one hundred and sixty thousand dollars,* she thought.

Stevie put the truck in gear and drove down the lane. "Over there," he pointed, "was a meth lab. When I inherited the land, I had it bulldozed."

"Was it your meth lab?" she asked, afraid of the answer.

"No, it was my father's."

"Can you answer me one thing. You said that there was a rumor about you and Katz? What was it?"

"That we're having an affair."

"Are you?" Rachael asked abruptly.

"Nope. She's a friend, a very good friend. I even took a bullet for her." Stevie held up his hand and showed his scar.

"I have a feeling there's a lot about you I need to know."

"Like my tabloid-worthy secrets," he laughed, stopping the truck. "I can let you in on a little secret right now."

"What? I'm all ears."

"Come closer so you can hear me," he whispered.

Rachael leaned in.

Stevie took the back of her head and pulled her toward him. He kissed her several times, then she kissed him back.

Chapter Eleven

Meanwhile at Rachael's Storefront

"Marko" Bruno, the hitman the New Jersey mob assigned to track down Emma, couldn't believe his luck. Finding her was a piece of cake. After identifying her outside the place where she lived, he checked out the guy she was talking to. He looked like a blond-haired country hick. Marko drove around the block. Heading back to where he sighted Emma, he saw her climbing into a red Dodge Ram with the hick. He discreetly followed them for a few miles, then assumed they were headed somewhere and wouldn't be back to the building in a while. He backtracked and parked in a parking lot behind her building. He identified which gate was Emma's and put his breaking-and-entering skills to use.

He broke into the courtyard, then kicked open the rear door. He began to search kitchen drawers, looking for the pink flash drive. When he found the drawers empty, he walked over to the laptop sitting on top of the butcher block island. He picked it up and scrutinized it, looking for a port where the flash drive could fit. Not finding one, he set the computer down and made a mental note to take it with him when he left.

He walked into the front of the storefront, looked around, and found nothing but a nightlight sitting on a bistro table.

He moved upstairs to the second floor. The kitchen and living room were devoid of furniture. There were dirty dishes in the sink, nothing in the refrigerator, except a bottle of seltzer water. Annoyed at not finding anything of interest, he climbed the stairs to the third floor. In the smaller bedroom there wasn't a stick of furniture and the closet was empty. In the larger bedroom there was an air mattress on the floor. The closet held only the bare necessities of a person who hadn't lived there very long. There were no clothes hanging up, but on the floor a suitcase lay. He picked it up and threw it on the mattress. Then he opened it and dumped the contents on the bed.

He rummaged through Emma's clothes and toiletries. Searching diligently, he was frustrated he didn't find the flash drive. Annoyed and in a fit of rage, he threw the empty suitcase across the room.

He stood in front of the window, which faced the street and looked below for the Dodge Ram. Not seeing it, he called his boss.

When the boss answered, Marko explained, "I found her. She's living in a three-story building on Main Street in Erie. I searched her place, but I didn't find the flash drive."

The boss yelled into the phone.

Marko moved the cell from his ear and waited for his boss to calm down, then said, "All right. I'll wait until she gets home, then I'll search her. I'll call you when it's done."

Marko didn't elaborate on what exactly *when it's done* meant. His job was to find the flash drive. He didn't know why it was so important to his boss. He wasn't curious enough to ask what was on it. He wasn't being paid to know. If he had to rough Emma up to get it, then so be it. If he had to kill her, he would.

He patted the butt of the handgun in his shoulder holster. He knew that if things got complicated, he'd have the necessary tool. He'd gotten the gun from a mob connection in Indy. In the back of his mind, he wondered why the guy in Indy wasn't hired to find this woman and why he had to fly from New Jersey to do the job. But it wasn't his place to question a direct order. It was all part of his job of creative problem-solving.

* * *

Gladys Kramer, a woman in her late sixties, lived in an apartment with her husband, Al. Their two-bedroom flat was on the third floor of a storefront on Erie's main street. Since she'd retired as a grade-school teacher, she was bored out of her mind. A friend recommended that she join the neighborhood watch group, whose members kept an eye out for criminal activities and contacted authorities if they suspected something. She agreed and had taken her civic duty seriously. She had nothing else to do. Al watched TV all day, and she passed the time looking out the picture window at the street below. Al called her gawking out the window spying; she called it surveillance.

Adjusting her thick-lensed glasses, Gladys spotted something of interest across the street at the third-floor building of the woman who had recently moved into town. She brought her binoculars up to her eyes and rotated the focus ring so she could get a better look at the man standing in front of the new owner's bedroom window.

Still viewing through the binoculars, she called to her husband, who was sitting in his recliner watching TV. "Al, something funny is going on across the street."

Al was used to his wife spying on everyone who lived on their block. He ignored the comment.

"Al, I said, there's a man standing in that new woman's bedroom."

"What new woman?"

"The one who's gonna open a café. She just moved here. She drives an old Toyota. You didn't notice her car when you parked your truck? It's in front of her building."

"Maybe it's her boyfriend."

"Why would a boyfriend be in her room, when she left with Stevie Sanders several hours ago."

"You mean the electrician?"

"Yes. He picked her up in his truck. They're not home yet."

"What's the man doing now?" the husband asked, punching a button to mute the TV.

"He's just standing there, talking on his phone. He keeps looking out and checking the street. I think he's up to no good. I'm calling the police."

"Gladys, we've been over this. The police are tired of your false alarms. Chief London said so himself."

"That's not true. The chief commended me for reporting those high school kids that were breaking into the shops."

"Call the non-emergency number," he suggested.

"Why?"

"So, you don't tie up 911 with your fairytale."

Chapter Twelve

Back at the Pink Mansion

Friday Evening

While Katherine sat in the living room on a blue wingback chair, her cell rang. The phone was stuck beside the chair's seat cushion, so she reached down and unwedged it. Putting the phone up to her ear, she didn't look to check the caller ID but assumed it was Jake, letting her know what time he'd be home. He was at the university attending a meeting regarding his new promotion. When he left, he said he didn't know how long the meeting would last. He suggested she eat dinner without him. She'd done that hours ago and was now watching her seven cats do what they always did before being put to bed. Abby and Iris were taking turns, rooting around in the lining under her chair. Nearby, Lilac was on the coffee table, leaning over like a vigilant vulture, watching them. Dewey and Crowie were taking turns batting a pink object across the wood floor. And last but not least, Scout and Abra were off doing their routine reconnaissance of the house before their bedtime.

"Hello," Katherine repeated.

"KC?" a sad voice asked.

"Salina, are you okay? It's nine o'clock. I thought you'd be asleep by now."

"Can I come over and talk to you?" Salina asked.

"Yes, of course, but please let your dad know."

"He's not home. He went over to see Rachael and hasn't come home yet."

"Well, at least text him or leave him a note that you're coming over. Oh, and Salina, it's getting dark. I'll come out and meet you halfway."

"Thanks, KC. Coming now."

Katherine rose from her chair and announced to the cats, "Salina's coming over. I want everyone to be on their best behavior."

"Yowl," Iris disagreed.

Katherine opened the door to meet Salina part of the way, but the teen was already on the porch. "You must have flown," she said.

Salina nodded.

"Come in. We're in the living room. Can I get you something to drink?"

"I'm good."

Katherine directed Salina to the second wingback chair and she sat down in the one she just vacated. "What's up?"

"Dad won't let me go to Julie's party Saturday night."

"The slumber party you were telling me about?"

"Yes. He's really mad at me."

"What happened?"

"I'll show you." Salina fished out her phone and found the video she submitted to YouTube. She pressed the start arrow and passed the phone to Katherine.

Katherine watched the entire video in stunned silence. She handed the phone back to Salina. "I didn't see you filming Rachael's reaction to the Siamese. Have you shown it to anyone else?"

Salina proceeded to elaborate how Shelly and she had uploaded it to YouTube and it had gone viral. "It was even shown on national news."

"I didn't see it," Katherine said. "Is this why your dad is angry at you?"

Salina blurted, "He made me go over and apologize to Rachael and she made me delete it."

"On your phone? But you just showed it to me."

"No, not on my phone. Rachael made me delete it from YouTube."

"I can see why your dad is annoyed."

"I thought he'd be proud of me," Salina said with a tear forming in her eye.

"Salina, your dad is very proud of you. I am, too. You said that you want to go to college to be a journalist?"

"Yes."

"A good journalist will ask the person she's interviewing if she can publish their photo or video."

Salina sighed. "I know, but I thought you would have at least taken my side."

"I agree with your dad on this one. Is Rachael mad at you, too?"

Salina rolled her eyes. "Gosh, KC, that's not even her real name. I Googled it. Her name is Emma Thomas. And you were right. She was Scout's and Abra's cat wrangler."

Katherine winked. "I seem to remember that you came up with the name cat wrangler," then added, "When she left my house, the other day, I looked online to find out information about her." She didn't tell Salina that she hadn't Googled Rachael Thomas because one of the cats did it for her. She'd gone to her office and found Abra in the vicinity of her computer. When Abra saw her, she leapt off the desk and ran out of the room. On the computer screen was a newspaper article about Emma Thomas, a professional cat wrangler, whose career ended when Harry DeSutter fired her, after one of his cat performers was stolen. Katherine said, "When Rachael worked for the magician, her name was Emma Thomas."

"So why is she telling people her name is Rachael?"

"Here's a thought, maybe when Emma moved to Erie she wanted to go by a different name. Maybe Rachael is her first or middle name. I don't think we need to make a big deal out of it."

"Oh, really?" Salina asked suspiciously. "I think dad should know the name of the woman he's dating."

A loud commotion occurred under Katherine's chair. Two cats were tussling. One yowled loudly, the other one hissed. The cat fight spilled out to the middle of the living room floor.

"Abby! Iris! Stop it right now!" Katherine demanded.

Abby had something clamped in her jaws. Iris tried to snatch it away, but Abby clenched it tighter. The battle over the stolen loot continued.

Katherine launched off her chair. "Drop it! Let me have it!"

Abby didn't oblige.

"Give it to me." Katherine reached down and gently tugged it out of Abby's jaw.

She gazed at the dog-eared photograph of the chief's wife, Connie. Then she caught a glimpse of Iris slinking behind the chair. "I know it was you, Fredo," she accused the blue-eyed thief.

Iris yowled sneakily.

Salina jumped up. "What is it?"

The laminated photo slipped out of Katherine's hand and fell to the floor.

Scout and Abra came into the room and trotted over to it. They began their death dance. Scout arched her back and began hopping up and down. Abra mimicked Scout's movements. They each yowled a long, drawn-out, banshee wail. Scout's pupils were mere slits; Abra was foaming spittle at the side of her jaw.

Salina pleaded, "KC, do something?"

Salina started to go to the cats, but Katherine grabbed her arm. "Don't. They're in some sort of trance. They might attack you."

"Cadabra, stop!" Katherine yelled Scout's former stage name, which in the past had good results in stopping the behavior. She snapped her fingers. "Cadabra, snap out of it."

The other cats freaked out and bolted out of the room, pounding the steps as they raced upstairs to their playroom safety zone.

Scout shook her head and sat down on her haunches. Abra licked Scout's ears.

Katherine moved over to pet them. "My darlings, are you okay now?"

"Raw," Abra said.

"Ma-waugh," Scout added.

There was a nervous silence, then Salina asked, "Why did they do that?"

"If I explain it to you, will you promise to not publish it on social media?"

Salina frowned. "Of course not."

"Do you know what a premonition is?"

"Like when you get a feeling that something bad is going to happen to someone."

"Yes, exactly. I've seen this behavior in the past. I won't go into details, but usually something bad does happen."

Salina retrieved the photo from the floor. "Do you think something bad is going to happen to this woman?"

Katherine shook her head. "I hope not. She's a good friend of mine."

"I've never seen her before."

"Yes, you have. You've just forgotten. She's the chief's wife, Connie."

"Chief London?"

Katherine nodded.

"What do we do? Call and warn her?" Salina fretted.

Katherine sat back down. "I'll take care of it tomorrow. I'll personally deliver the stolen picture to the chief."

"Won't he get mad?"

"No, he'll chuckle about it. He knows that Iris is a thief."

"How did she get ahold of it?"

"She's a pickpocket."

Salina snickered. "When was he here last?"

"A few days ago." She smiled, remembering the cat-under-the-table incident, and how during the meeting, Iris had probably stolen the photo.

"Well, okay. I'm going to go home now."

"I'll walk you home."

"Cool."

Katherine hugged her and the two walked outside.

The shrill keening of the cicadas was temporarily blocked by the blaring sirens of a number of emergency vehicles racing down Highway 41.

Salina asked, "I wonder what that's about?"

"They're probably first responders to a fire somewhere."

Suddenly Salina worried about the whereabouts of her dad, whose truck wasn't parked in front of the house. "KC, he's not back."

"No worries. I'm sure he'll be home soon."

"Okay, thanks for walking me home."

"Anytime."

"Love ya, KC."

"Love ya, too!"

Chapter Thirteen

On Friday evening, Chief London was on duty. He'd already arrested a drunk who was driving on the wrong side of the road. He'd broken up a fight at the ice cream stand. Two acne-faced teens were fighting over a girl who didn't look a day over thirteen. When he answered the radio call from the emergency dispatcher — his niece Maureen — he was abrupt. "Did you say Gladys Kramer called this in? Egad, I wonder what she's reporting now."

"Breaking and entering in progress. 404 Main Street. The suspect is on the third floor of the building across the street from Gladys. She said the owner, Rachael Thomas, was not at home. She said the man keeps looking down at the street as if he's looking for her to come back."

"Someone needs to do me a favor and take away her binoculars."

The dispatcher laughed.

"I'm on my way," he affirmed.

The chief didn't need to punch in the address on his GPS. He already knew where Rachael Thomas lived. He drove his Erie town police cruiser and parked in front of the storefront. He observed an older model Toyota parked in front as well. He ran the plates. He said out loud, "She's legal." Then he checked the BMV online vehicle registration. The owner was an LLC, but the address was Rachael Thomas's. *Interesting*, he thought.

Before the chief got out of the cruiser, he radioed for assistance from Officer Troy, who was also on duty. He advised him to park in the back of the building. "Gladys Kramer reported this, so don't expect to find anything, but we need to check it out anyway. I'll go in the front and you go in the back, that is, if we can get in."

"Got it," Officer Troy confirmed.

The chief scanned the street for pedestrians, but the block was quiet, except for the restaurant patrons going in and out of the hotel. He tried the front glass door of the storefront, but it was locked. He wasn't surprised. *You'd be a damned fool if you didn't lock your doors in this age*, he thought. He cupped his hands and peered through the window. The owner had a nightlight on a bistro table. He scanned the room but didn't see anything suspicious.

Across the street, Gladys observed the chief parking in front of the storefront. "Why isn't his siren on?" she grumbled. She followed him with her eyes as he walked to the front of the shop. "Why isn't he going inside?" she voiced.

Al wasn't listening. He was watching his favorite TV show.

"Al, pay attention, the chief's here."

"Here?"

"He just parked in front of that woman's place."

"Yeah, it's a tragedy," Al said non-committedly.

"Wait! He's getting in his car and leaving. What the heck? Why in the world?" she complained.

* * *

The chief climbed in his cruiser and drove to the rear of the building. He parked next to Officer Troy's vehicle. He noticed that the gate to the owner's courtyard was standing wide open. Knowing Officer Troy was already in the building, he cautiously walked in, constantly looking back and forth for signs of criminal activity.

The back door was open as well. Before the chief entered, he shouted a warning, "Police!" He moved inside, scanning the room. Satisfied there wasn't anything amiss, he found the stairs to the second floor. He looked for a light switch but couldn't find one. He stopped in his tracks when he heard the gunshots. Two shots were fired, and the sound of a body collapsing on the floor above. He prayed it wasn't Officer Troy.

The chief unstrapped his service revolver and held it with both hands in an aimed-to-shoot stance. He slowly took each stair one at a time.

At the turn in the staircase, a man rushed down the steps and pushed him. The chief fell back but caught himself on the railing. "Halt," he yelled at the man, "Or I'll shoot." The man kept running. The chief fired a warning shot. The man stopped, turned and fired back. The bullet hit Chief London in the chest. The impact jarred him to his bones and knocked the wind out of him. He teetered into the railing and crumpled on the steps, then lost consciousness.

On the third floor, Officer Troy had sustained two wounds in his right hand and shoulder. He tried to bring his injured hand up to radio for help but the pain was too much. In shock, he fainted.

* * *

Gladys brought the binoculars up to her eyes and stared at the third-floor window. "I don't see that guy anymore." She stood looking for several more minutes, then she saw the flash of two gunshots. She heard a third. "Al! Al! Oh, my word. Somebody's been shot."

Al rose from his recliner and rushed over. "I heard it. Three blasts. Get on the phone, woman, and call it in."

Gladys grabbed her cell and punched in 911. She shouted into the phone, "Send him back. Send him back." Gladys struggled to find the right words to report to the dispatcher what she'd seen.

The dispatcher tried to calm her down.

Finally, Gladys composed herself and said, "I heard three gunshots from across the street at that building at 404 Main. Chief London came and then left. Tell him to come back. Hurry!"

"Ma'am, hold the line. My board is lighting up." While the dispatcher put Gladys on hold, she alerted the proper authorities.

Gladys grew impatient and hung up. "Al, we have to go over there."

"Why on earth would we want to do that?"

"Because when the chief comes back, we have to warn him that the gunman is inside that storefront. We have to let him know."

"That's nuts. We could get shot!"

"I'm going."

"Stop! You've done your civic duty. Let's wait until the coast is clear, then we'll go over there."

Gladys didn't listen to him. She rushed out of their apartment and slammed the door.

* * *

After the shooting, Marko walked over to the chief and stared down at him. Satisfied that the chief wasn't getting up, he didn't put another bullet in him. He wanted to, but he'd already fired three shots. The top floor cop didn't have time to fire his weapon, but the cop on the first floor did. That many shots would have alerted someone on the street or in one of the neighboring buildings. His car was in the rear parking lot. He didn't want to risk getting caught by retrieving his car from there. And even if he wanted to, it would be a fool's mission, because he suddenly heard sirens wailing in the distance.

He exited the storefront through the front door. He walked to a nearby Toyota Tercel and tried to open the door. Finding it locked, he went to the pickup truck parked in front of it and tried its door. It wasn't locked. He looked around for any witnesses. When he didn't see anybody, he jumped in. The owner had left the keys above the driver's side sun visor. "Stupid hick didn't even lock his truck!" he said, starting the vehicle. He put it in gear, stomped on the accelerator, and sped out of town.

Once out of Erie, he pounded his fists on the steering wheel. "Damn, I so screwed up. I have to fix this before the boss finds out," he said angrily.

* * *

"That woman drives me crazy," Al muttered, looking out the window, contemplating whether or not he should follow his wife. He yanked his phone out of his hip pocket and punched in her number. He wanted to tell her to wait, and that he'd be there as soon as he put on his shoes. When he spotted a man leaving the building, he said, "Well, looky there!" He tapped his phone to camera mode and took several high-resolution pictures. *Isn't Gladys going to be jealous of me when I give the pics to the chief? A photo beats out an oral description of a criminal any day.* Well, he assumed the man was the one who fired the shots. Although it was suspicious that the man tried to open the old Toyota's door, but obviously it was locked. Al wasn't completely convinced until he saw the man get into his pickup.

"Holy Toledo! He's stealin' my truck!"

Chapter Fourteen

A few hours earlier, Stevie and Rachael had driven to Chester's barbecue kiosk. Stevie thought it would be fun to eat their sandwiches while sitting by one of the wind turbines on his property. He turned off the paved road, onto a concrete pad, and parked. Nearby was the large, circular base of a turbine. "This is a good place," he said.

They both climbed out of the truck. Rachael was holding the bags of food while Stevie fetched two lawn chairs from the back of his truck. "Oh, wait before we eat," he said, heading back to his truck. He grabbed a can of mosquito spray and returned. "The flying vampires are out tonight," he joked, handing the can to Rachael. She sprayed her arms, then Stevie did the same. They sat down and ate their barbecue. When they'd finished, they talked: Stevie first; then Rachael.

They talked about every topic under the sun, except about those people who might be incriminated and hurt their chances for a relationship.

Stevie even discussed, at length, his criminal past. Rachael listened. She didn't offer criticism or rebuke him in any way. In turn, Rachael talked about her life, her many majors at school, her difficulty finding the right guy, and about her grandmother's cancer. She skipped over her short stint of being a cat wrangler, and Stevie didn't ask for more information. What she didn't mention was that she was a criminal herself. Not an ex-criminal like Stevie, but a thief who had stolen a digital ledger from a mob boss, and thousands of dollars in cash from her ex-fiancé. Instead, Rachael ended the conversation with a comment about it getting late.

"Is it?" Stevie said, looking at his watch. "I guess it is."

"And getting dark," she said, swiping a hungry mosquito from her face.

"Okay, but before we leave, I want you to do something for me?"

"What?" she asked, studying his face for a clue of what he wanted.

"Look up at the turbine's lights."

Rachael stood up and looked. Each turbine flicked a series of red flashes. "Amazing," she said in awe. "It looks like a million fireflies."

"The lights are warning lights for pilots flying overhead."

"Makes sense."

"Here's something else that makes sense," Stevie said getting up. He pulled her into an embrace. "I really want to do this again."

"Me, too," Rachael said, hugging him back. She thought, *I've changed my mind. I'm not leaving Erie tomorrow. I'm going to call Ray and meet him somewhere. I'll hand over the flash drive and the money, and be done with it.*

"One more kiss for the road?" Stevie asked tenderly.

Rachael smiled.

He took her face in his hands and kissed her a sweet gentle kiss.

"Thank you for everything," she said.

"You bet."

Then the couple grabbed their lawn chairs and walked to the truck. Stevie took both chairs and put them on the truck bed. Rachael climbed into the cab.

They drove back to Erie in silence, holding hands.

On the outskirts of the town, Stevie and Rachael noticed an ambulance shrieking by. A second one followed.

"What the hell?" Stevie asked.

"What's going on?"

"Something big. There must have been a bad wreck."

They drove into town. Main Street was blocked by several state and local police cars. An Erie cop Stevie didn't recognize motioned for Stevie to stop. He came over to the truck. Stevie powered his window down. "Officer, what's the problem here?" he asked.

Rachael could see the large police presence in front of her building. The color drained from her face.

The officer said, "This is an active crime scene. You'll have to turn back."

Rachael squeezed Stevie's hand as hard as she could.

He glanced over at her, saw her shake her head, and mouth the word "no." Then he realized she didn't want the cop to know it was her building.

He answered, "Thanks. Will do."

He put the truck in gear and backed up. He then headed back out-of-town.

"What was that about?" he asked Rachael.

She didn't answer.

"Why didn't you want the cop to know you lived there?"

"I can't say."

"Yes, you can." Stevie turned down a country road, pulled over and parked. "Listen, I've known from the very first time I met you that you're afraid of something."

"How would you know that?"

"Because you freaked out when Intruder came into your house. A normal person would have checked it out, or hid."

"That's what I did. I hid!"

"You cowered in the corner like a trapped animal. Then my daughter posted that video of you that made national news. I watched your reaction. You looked like you were going to run out of the building, jump in your car, and leave town. Am I right?"

"Yes," Rachael whispered.

"I have a strong suspicion it's someone you know. Someone you had a relationship with. Someone who has threatened to hurt you."

Rachael began to cry.

Stevie got out of the truck and came to her side. He opened the door and extended his hand to her. "Come here," he said.

"I can't."

"You can. I want to hold you."

"My knees are knocking."

He reached up and helped her out. He hugged her and held her for a moment, then said, "Something really bad happened back there at your place. Someone probably got seriously injured. You need to get it together because I'm taking you back so you can talk to the cops."

"I can't. I can't. I have to run. Please help me."

"Run from what?"

"My ex-fiancé is a gangster," she blurted out. "He said that if I ever left him, he'd kill me. I think he knows where I live."

"Wait. Back up a step. Where does he live?"

"In Atlantic City, New Jersey."

"Well, that's a long way from here. When you left him, did you leave a paper trail of where he could find you?"

"No, I made sure of that when I left. I covered all the bases. I didn't tell my friends where I was going. I didn't tell my Grammy. I didn't leave any kind of forwarding address. I had it planned out to the last detail. I made myself disappear."

"So, what do you have to be afraid of?"

"I wasn't afraid until Salina's video went viral."

"I'm so sorry that happened."

"What am I going to do? If I go back to my place, he could be lurking in the shadows ready to catch me."

"You can come home with me."

"No, that's a terrible idea. What if he follows us? You have Salina to think of."

"Okay. Okay. Let me think." Stevie thought for a moment, then said, "I'll go with you when you talk to the cops."

"No. I'm not talking to the police," she said adamantly.

"Your place is crawling with cops. Your ex would be an idiot to show up now."

"What do you mean?"

"You'll be protected as long as the cops are there. But first, we need to find out what happened. I'm bankin' it had nothing to do with your ex showing up. I'll call my brother."

"Why your brother?"

"Half-brother," Stevie corrected. "Dave owns the tavern at the edge of town."

"So?"

"In this town, if you want to find out anything you either hang out at the Red House diner, or have a drink at the Dew Drop Inn."

"Small town," Rachael observed.

Dave answered on the third ring. "What's up, bro?"

Stevie put the call on speaker. "Do you know what's goin' on Main Street? The place looks like a cop convention."

"Yeah, I heard a couple of cops were shot in that building next to the Erie Hotel."

"Shot?" Stevie said, shocked. He looked over at Rachael. Her jaw dropped.

"Heard it was pretty bad. One of them had to be airlifted to Indy."

"Are you talkin' about the place where I did the electrical work?"

"Yeah, belongs to the woman who wants to open a café."

"Did you hear if the shooter was caught?"

"No, he got away."

"Well, thanks for the intel."

"Stop in and see me sometime."

"Will do." Stevie ended the call and turned to Rachael.

She spoke first. "Oh, this is terrible. I can't believe this is happening." She buried her face in her hands.

"I wonder why the cops were at your place?"

"I don't know," she shook her head. "But I do know Ray shot them and got away. Now he's going to be coming after me."

Stevie tried to defuse the situation by asking a question. "So, Ray is your ex's name?"

"His name is Ray Russo."

"When I did time, I knew a Russo. He was Italian."

"Ray is *very* Italian."

"What do you mean by *very* Italian? I ain't from New Jersey."

"He's Sicilian."

"Dang, girl, you surprise me every day."

"Not all Italians or Sicilians are criminals," she defended. "Some of my close friends are Italian, and trust me, they are good people."

"Good people, but not your fiancé?"

"Ex."

"All right, let's get back on track. Here's the plan. I'll take you back home. We'll talk to whoever is in charge, tell them the honest truth—"

"No way," Rachael protested. "I'm not telling them about Ray."

"Why would you have to? In my experience, as a former criminal, you never volunteer anything to the cops. Got that?"

"Yes."

"You'll say you were on a date with me. True fact. Describe the barbecue food, tell them what we've been doing for the last few hours."

"Okay, I'll try, but I'm so nervous, I'm not sure I can do that."

"If that happens, then I'll tell it for you. You don't have to worry. I'll be there to back up what you say."

"Then what? I've watched enough crime shows to know the police are not going to let me back inside my place until they've processed the crime scene." Rachael's voice broke. "How am I going to get my car? I need to pick up Intruder tomorrow."

"We'll figure out something."

"Where are we going to live? We can't stay at the hotel. That's too close."

"I'll take you to a safe place where Ray won't find you. And if he does, he'll have hell to pay."

"Where? What do you mean, hell to pay?"

"My friend Ted lives way out in the woods."

"But I don't know him," she said apprehensively. "Is there anywhere else I can stay the night?"

"Don't worry. Ted has been a friend for a very long time. Trust me. No one will mess with him."

"Why is that?" she asked, still not convinced staying with a stranger out in the middle of nowhere was a safe idea.

"He's a part-time bouncer. He's big and fearless, and won't be afraid to protect anyone I care about."

Rachael burst into more tears. "I'm so sorry I've brought this to your door."

Chapter Fifteen

After Katherine walked Salina home, she returned to the mansion and decided to wait up for Jake. Scout and Abra stood tall on the turret's window sill. Dewey and Crowie were in the atrium, sitting on the bottom step. Lilac and Abby were somewhere else. Iris trotted in and threw herself against Katherine's leg. She mourned a sad yowl.

Katherine picked her up. "What's wrong, sweetheart?"

Iris yowled again and buried her face in Katherine's neck. Katherine cuddled her for a moment, then said, "Miss Siam, I have to set you down now. I need to feed you guys and put you to bed."

Katherine's cats were creatures of routine. As soon as she said the words "feed you guys," Lilac and Abby appeared from the back of the house and bounded up the stairs. Dewey and Crowie were a fast third and fourth. Then Scout and Abra raced by. Only Iris remained behind.

Katherine picked her up and carried her to the playroom, where the other cats had gathered around their porcelain Haviland bowls. She gave each cat a small cup of dry kibble, fluffed up their cozy beds, then locked them in. Before she shut the door, she counted cats. "Yep, all seven accounted for. Good night, my treasures."

The cats were too busy eating to answer, except for Dewey, who bellowed a loud "Mao."

"You're welcome," she answered.

Iris stood by her bowl but wasn't interested in her food.

"Miss Siam, if you don't eat your food, the other cats will."

Iris yowled sadly.

Katherine went downstairs and headed to the kitchen. She poured herself a glass of cabernet, then went back to the living room and sat down in the wingback chair. Putting her phone down on the coffee table, she sipped on her wine.

A few minutes later, Jake came home. He opened the front door and called for her, "Katz, are you still up?"

"I'm in the living room," she said, watching him walk in.

"Hi, handsome," she said with a smile.

He had a serious look on his face. He came over to her chair and got down on his knees. He took her hands into his.

"Jake, what's wrong?"

"Daryl called me."

"Daryl? Is he okay? Is something wrong with Colleen?"

"They're fine. Katz, I have some bad news."

"What? Tell me?"

"Chief London has been shot."

Katherine covered her mouth with her hand. "Oh, no."

"Daryl is on his way to Erie. Sheriff Johnson called in a few men to help keep law and order in town."

"Is the chief in critical condition?" Katherine couldn't contain her sobs and broke down.

Standing up, Jake said, "Katz, get up. Come sit with me." He offered his hand and helped her up. He led her to a nearby loveseat.

"Daryl didn't know. He said the chief and one of his officers were responding to a break in at Rachael Thomas's place—"

"Rachael's place," she repeated. "Why would anyone want to do that? Was she home when it happened?"

Jake shook his head. "Don't know."

"What else did Daryl say?"

"That's it, except one of the officers had to be helicoptered to Indy. He said he didn't know which one."

"I know it was the chief. I just know it."

Jake gave her an inquisitive look. "How would you know that?"

She picked up the photo of the chief's wife and passed it to Jake. She then explained why she had it and who had stolen it.

"Coincidence, Katz. Iris is a master of picking pockets."

"Yes, Iris is a thief, but a few minutes ago, when I put the cats to bed, she was troubled about something. I had to hold and comfort her, then when the other cats were bolting down their food, like they do, she just stood by her bowl and didn't eat."

"What would Iris be troubled about?"

"She really likes the chief."

"Oh," Jake said. "You're right, but it's Scout and Abra who predict things."

"Like tonight."

"What do they have to do with the chief being shot?"

"After I grabbed the photo from Abby—"

"You mean Iris."

"No, Abby had the photo. Iris was fighting her to get it. Scout and Abra came into the room, took one look at the photo, and started doing their death dance. Hopping up and down like deranged Halloween cats. I assumed something terrible was going to happen to Connie, not the chief."

"I see the connection now."

"When did Daryl call you?"

"About a half hour ago."

"Call him back. By now, he should know more about what's going on."

"Katz, Daryl can't release ongoing official police business."

"Oh, come on, Jake," Katherine said, annoyed. "He can at least tell us which hospital Chief London is in, or if he's dead or alive?"

"Katz, listen, Daryl can't tell us anything until the higher-ups say he can."

"Higher-ups? Who's in charge if Chief London isn't able to do the job?"

"I assume Sheriff Johnson."

"This is frustrating. I'd text Connie, but I don't know her cell number."

"I'm sure she's been notified. She's probably right by his side."

Katherine started to cry again. "He's my friend. I love him."

Jake hugged her. "Talk it out, Katz."

"When I first moved here, he was one of the first people I met. He was the officer who responded to my call about Vivian Marston. He pronounced her dead."

"I know, sweet pea."

"When my house was damaged by the tornado, and I was staying at the bungalow, do you know what Connie and he did?"

"No. Tell me."

"Connie made him bring me over something for my breakfast. It was so thoughtful. And over the years, I've really gotten to know him. I just can't . . . can't . . ." Her voice trembled and trailed off into silence.

"Katz, maybe it was the other officer who was airlifted."

"Hang on a minute," she said, retrieving her cell. She texted Margie a message about what Jake had just told her about the chief. Knowing how gifted Margie was at getting information, she'd probably know the full story by now.

Margie texted back. *"Officer Troy was airlifted to Indy; Chief London was taken to the ER at the hospital across the bridge. I'll text you if I learn anything else."*

"Thanks," Katherine answered.

She relayed the message to Jake. "Let's go there. He's in the ER in that hospital across the bridge. I can't sit here not knowing if he's okay or not."

"Let's go. Get your purse," Jake said, leaving.

"I'll meet you outside."

Chapter Sixteen

The hitman, Marko Bruno, was fifty miles away from Erie before he called his boss. He needed time to come up with a good excuse for why he hadn't gotten the ledger. He pulled over at a gas station, went inside to get a cup of coffee, and then returned to the stolen truck. He punched in his boss's number and counted the seconds before the boss would blow up.

Marko was pleasantly surprised that his boss didn't blow up. Even when he told him about the two cops he'd shot. The boss simply clicked off a bunch of instructions of what he should do next, which he already knew by heart, because he'd done this kind of job so many times before. His orders were to dump the gun in the closest body of water. Check. He'd already done that by throwing it in the Wabash River on the way out of town. He was instructed to drive the stolen vehicle to the Indy airport, park it in long-term parking, then get on the shuttle to catch his plane. Check, sort of. Marko had two stolen vehicles. One was parked in the back of the storefront. And the other he was driving.

The boss said to text him when he got to the airport in Atlantic City. He'd arrange for somebody to pick him up. Check. That was easy enough.

Hanging up, Marko said, "Piece of cake."

Because Marko wasn't the sharpest knife in the drawer, he didn't pick up on the subliminal message from the new personality assumed by his normally tough-as-nails boss. The light would come on later for Marko, when the guy who would pick him up would drive the hitman to an abandoned house and, as instructed, snuff him out.

The boss wasn't playing. He called Ray and asked him to finish the job.

Chapter Seventeen

Stevie parked his pickup a block from the hotel. Rachael sat quietly in the passenger seat. She hadn't said a word since they started back to Erie.

Stevie climbed out and went to her door. Opening it, he said, "Are you ready? Do I need to coach you anymore?"

"No, I'm fine. Let's get this over with." She got out and joined him on the sidewalk.

The street in front of the hotel and storefront was cordoned off with yellow police tape. Two deputies stood behind the tape, checking identifications. They were turning people away. Stevie suspected those people were nosy Erie folk trying to find out what happened. Stevie recognized the first deputy. It was Daryl Cokenberger — the man who'd shot and killed Stevie's father, and the one who apprehended a murderer on the beach at Lake Michigan. "Yep, small town," Stevie mumbled.

Daryl recognized Stevie with a nod. "Mr. Sanders, I need to see your ID. Ma'am, I need to see yours, also."

Rachael dug her driver's license out of her purse, and handed it to Daryl. "I own the storefront next to the

Erie Hotel. What's going on?" She didn't want the deputy to know she already knew two cops had been shot.

"Rachael Thomas," Daryl said, scrutinizing the license, then looking up at her when she spoke. "You need to follow me."

"You didn't answer my question," she said boldly. Stevie nudged her.

"There's been an incident. The state police detective needs to talk to you."

Stevie asked, "She's with me. Can I come, too?"

"Yeah, sure. I see no problem with that. Follow me. I'll take you to her."

Detective Linda Martin stood finishing up notes she'd taken after talking to Gladys Kramer. Her ears were burning from Gladys's rambling monologue of what happened, which included details that had nothing to do with the case. She was used to witnesses like Gladys. Stress and shock can wear down the most reliable witness. However, she wasn't used to her husband's account. Getting information from him was a slow, difficult process. Al, like his wife, was very descriptive, but most of it had nothing to do with the case. Finally, Al got to the important facts: The suspect stole his pickup and, as icing on the cake, Al had taken two photos of the man who committed the crime.

The detective helped Al airdrop the photos to her phone, then she said both of them could go home. She handed each one her state police card and asked them to call if they could think of anything else.

In the meantime, Stevie and Rachael walked up. Daryl introduced Rachael, but not Stevie. Everyone in the area knew who Stevie Sanders was.

Gladys returned from across the street, yelling. "That's her! That's her! Rachael Thomas." She waved like a hysterical winner on a TV game show.

Detective Martin said, "Mrs. Kramer, I have this under control. Please go home now."

Rachael said to Stevie, "How does that woman know my name?"

Stevie said in a low voice, "She's the town's busybody."

Gladys ignored the detective and continued, "Rachael, a man broke into your place and shot two of our finest. My husband took pictures of him. Want to see them? Al show her your phone?"

"Mrs. Kramer, I said go home," the detective said sharply. Then when it became obvious that Gladys was not budging from her spot, the detective said, "Deputy, escort this couple home."

"Yes, ma'am," Daryl said, with one hand on Gladys' arm and the other on Al's.

Al shucked Daryl's hand away. "No need to get touchy feely," he groused.

Rachael said, "I have the right to know what's going on. Who are you?"

"I'm Detective Linda Martin with the Indiana State Police. I'm working this case. Stevie, what's your connection to Rachael?"

Stevie put his arm around Rachael. "We're a couple."

Rachael looked up at him curiously.

Detective Martin's eyes grew round in surprise, then she went back to her professional manner. Stevie had a history of dating a long line of women whose relationships went nowhere. She was hoping Stevie had found someone at last.

"Rachael, I have a few questions to ask you. What time did you leave your building?"

"Stevie picked me up at six or a little after."

Detective Martin proceeded to ask a lengthy list of routine questions, which Rachael answered honestly.

Stevie supported Rachael's every word, but added, "She's been with me. I picked her up at six. We went to Chester's kiosk and picked up dinner. We had a picnic on my property across the road. We headed back to Erie when it started to get dark."

"That's good to know," the detective said, then asked Rachael, "While you two were having a picnic across from Chester's, do you know why a man would be in your bedroom?"

"No."

The detective pulled up the photos she'd obtained from Al and showed them to Rachael. "Do you recognize this man?"

Rachael took a good look at each photo. She shook her head. "I've never seen him before." Inside, she was ecstatic with relief because the man wasn't Ray. He was probably some local thug breaking in to see if the new arrival in town had any cash or drugs around.

"Is there anything else you can tell me?"

"No, I can't think of anything. Can I ask you a question?"

"Sure."

"Can I go inside and get my things? I need my laptop."

"No, the scene is still being processed. We had two officers shot in your place. We are gathering evidence as to who shot them."

"I am so sorry about that."

Detective Martin said, "We *all* are sorry. Chief London and Officer Troy are remarkable men. Oh, by the way, Rachael, you can't stay here. You'll have to find somewhere else to live. You won't be able to come back until we're finished."

"I understand, but how long will that be?"

"Could be a few days or a few weeks. Once all the forensic evidence has been collected, I'll give you a call."

Stevie asked, "Are we finished? Can we leave now?"

The detective didn't answer, but said to Rachael, "I ask that you remain in the area. You're not planning on going out of town, are you?"

Stevie piped in, "Nope, she's not."

"Okay then, I'll need both of your cell phone numbers."

Stevie offered his, but Rachael didn't.

"Cell phone number, Rachael?" the detective asked again.

"It's a new phone. I'm not used to calling myself." Rachael fished in her purse and brought out the cell. She found the number and gave it to the detective.

The detective handed Rachael an official card. "If you can think of anything or have questions, please don't hesitate to call, text or email me. Thank you for your cooperation. Good night." The detective turned away and walked inside the storefront.

"Ma'am, good night to you, too," Stevie called after her, then took Rachael's arm. "Let's get out of here."

"What about my car?"

Stevie glanced over at the Tercel. "I'd leave it here until the police are gone, then you can get it."

"I only want to repark it in the rear parking lot."

"Sweet girl, wait until tomorrow. Whether you know it or not, you're a person of interest."

"But I haven't done anything."

"I know that, and you know that, but all eyes will be on you until they find out who did this."

"Just for moving my car?"

"Yep. See those cops over there? One of them will jump in his vehicle and follow you. Do you really want the hassle of answering more questions just to park your car?"

"Oh, I get it. The cops will think I'm fleeing the area."

"Yep, but keep on walkin'. The quicker we get out of here, the less chance the detective will come back and ask more questions."

"You win."

"Let's get you to Ted's."

"Stevie," she hesitated, then said, "I don't have any clothes."

"Unfortunately, there aren't any stores in Erie open right now. You'll have to wait until tomorrow."

Rachael stopped in front of the hotel. "There's no need for me to go to Ted's. I'll be safe here. Then I can keep a close eye on my storefront."

"I'm not sure that's a good idea."

"Why? The guy in the photos wasn't Ray. I don't have to worry anymore."

"Okay, I guess." Stevie climbed the hotel's front steps and opened the door. Rachael followed him. Once inside, he hugged her. "I'll call you in the morning."

Rachael smiled and headed to the front desk.

* * *

Later in her room, Rachael texted Stevie that she was on the second floor in room 217. She wished him a good night, thanked him again, and inserted a heart emoticon. Stevie promptly texted one back.

After she hung up her T-shirt and jeans, she showered and wrapped a bath towel around her. She found a binder clip in one of the drawers and fastened the top of the towel, because she'd have to wear it like pajamas. She'd make a note that tomorrow before she picked up Intruder, she'd go to the dollar store and buy several T-shirts and jeans.

"I need to write a list," she said aloud.

She grabbed her purse and looked for something to write on. She grumbled that the hotel was stingy in what they had in the room: No pen, no paper, not even a directory of their amenities except a battered sign that said Free Wi-Fi.

"Free Wi-Fi," she huffed. "Fat chance that's happening when my laptop is sitting on the kitchen counter back at the storefront."

Not finding anything to write on, she dumped her satchel purse on the bed. She found a pen and index card, then thought it wise to make sure the flash drive was safe and sound in the slotted part of her purse.

It wasn't there.

She removed every item, placing them on the nearby nightstand. No flash drive.

She panicked.

What happened to it? I know it's been in my purse. I've never moved it from that slot, she thought.

Then the worst thing came to mind. *What if it fell out somewhere in my storefront? What if the police found it? Then what?*

She envisioned herself being indicted along with every criminal on the ledger.

"Calm down. Take a deep breath," she said aloud.

Maybe the police won't find it, she thought. *Maybe they'll let me go back to my place soon. Maybe I'll be lucky and it'll be under the bed or in some ridiculous place they didn't check.*

She put the items back into her purse, lay down and covered herself with a summer-weight blanket. *I'm too tired to worry about this now.*

She couldn't sleep. Her mind raced with the events of the day, her past, her fears, and how much she was falling for Stevie. She couldn't wait to hold her kitten again.

Then she sat up in bed, wide-eyed with suspicion. Kitten? Cat? It was something Salina had said about Katherine Cokenberger's cats. Something about one or two of them being thieves and hiding stuff in an old chair. Rachael soon put two-and-two together. *One of Katz's cats got into my purse and stole the flash drive.*

Nah, that's ridiculous, her inner voice answered.

"No, not really. I was distracted when I saw Cadabra and Abra. Maybe one of the cats snuck underneath my chair and stole it then?"

The inner voice countered, *if one of them did, how are you going to get it back?*

"Maybe I could drive over and ask Katz if she'd found something that belonged to me. I'll tell her that it's my personal photo album backed up on a pink memory stick."

The inner voice scolded. *That would be stupid. You never lay your cards on the table.*

"Oh, shut up!" Rachael said. "And let me sleep."

Rachael nodded off before deciding on what she should do. It was too much to contemplate. Exhausted, she fell into a deep slumber.

Chapter Eighteen

When Jake and Katherine arrived at the hospital there were few parking spaces left. A large crowd had gathered at the ER's entrance door. A podium had been set up, and Sheriff Johnson stood behind it. The Channel 19 news station had cameras poised to record his statement. Reporters lined up in front to ask questions. Jake and Katherine took their places at the back of the group.

Sheriff Johnson spoke in a somber voice, "I wish to make this announcement."

A hush fell over the crowd; people pushed in to hear.

"Tonight, two of our finest were shot in the line of duty."

"How are they?" someone yelled from the crowd.

"Chief London is in stable condition. He was wearing a bulletproof vest. He sustained a shot to his chest. The impact of the bullet caused several of the chief's ribs to be bruised. The doctors are watching for signs of internal hemorrhage. He'll be held here at the hospital for further observation, and most likely will be released tomorrow."

"Yay," several people in the center of the group shouted.

"What about Officer Troy?" another person yelled.

"Officer Troy was helicoptered to an Indianapolis hospital. He sustained a wound to his hand and shoulder. He's in critical condition, but doctors are optimistic he will survive—"

Loud applause monetarily drowned out the Sheriff's speech.

Then he continued, "This is an ongoing investigation. The suspect is still at large." He held up a blown-up photo of the suspect. "If anyone knows who this is, or can give us any information about the case, please call the state police hotline or my office."

The reporters starting shouting a barrage of questions. The Sheriff put up his hand in a "stop" gesture. "That's all I have to report at this time."

He left the podium and walked in through the ER entrance.

People in the crowd lingered, until one of the guarding officers told them to disperse. "Thank you for coming. I'm sure the chief appreciates it. Let's go home, folks. We'll know more tomorrow."

Jake hugged Katherine. "Hopefully, whoever did this will be caught."

"I'm relieved the chief will be okay. I'm ready to go home," she said in a weary voice.

"Me, too."

When they drove into the pink mansion's driveway, Katherine was happy to see that Stevie's truck was parked in front of the Foursquare and the lights were off in his house. She hoped he'd reach out to her about what had transpired tonight and what Rachael's connection was. Not knowing the facts, she wondered what Chief London and Officer Troy were doing in Rachael's place to begin with.

She sighed. She hadn't really talked to Stevie in months, not since the autumn. She'd say hello when she saw him in his yard or about town. He'd be polite. She suspected that their friendship was waning.

Chapter Nineteen

Saturday Morning

When Rachael woke up and realized there wasn't a coffee maker in the room, she complained, "What should I expect? The hotel wants you to get coffee in the restaurant. I hope they're open, because I'm starved."

Her phone pinged. She picked it up off the bedside table. It was Stevie.

"*Hungry?*" he texted.

"*Famished*"

"*Be there in 5*"

"*Make it 20, just got up.*"

"*Ok.*"

She put her phone down, then picked it right back up. She called the vet to see what time she could come and get Intruder. The receptionist answered and said the kitten could be released any time in the morning, before noon.

"Okay, thanks."

Then Rachael called the hotel's front desk. "Hi. My name is Rachael Thomas. I'm in room 217. I forgot to mention last night that I'll be staying up to two weeks. Can you book me the same room I'm in for that amount of time?"

"Yes, we can."

"I also forgot to ask, are you a pet-friendly hotel?"

"Only if the animal is a service animal."

"Meaning you don't allow pets."

"Nope. Is that a problem?"

"Yes. I have a kitten."

"Is the kitten with you now?" the woman shrieked into the phone as if the kitten were bringing in a case of the plague.

"No, she's not."

"Well, I'm sorry then, we're not allowed to accommodate you if you have a pet."

"Okay. I'll be checking out soon," she said, frustrated. Rachael ended the call. She wished it had been on the landline so she could have slammed the receiver down. She criticized, "This place is a dump. What could my darling possibly do to make it worse?"

"Ridiculous!" she grumbled, throwing on her clothes. She ran a brush through her hair and tied it up with a scrunchie. She was finishing up when there was a knock on the door.

She opened it wide, thinking it was Stevie. "What took you so long?" she teased.

"Ma'am?" Detective Martin asked. "I take it you're expecting someone else?"

Rachael was caught off guard, then hid her shock at seeing the detective so soon after the previous night. She didn't answer the question. "Can I help you?"

"May I come in?"

"Sure. I haven't had time to make my bed yet. We could sit over here." Rachael directed the detective to a small table and two chairs.

The detective placed her laptop on the table and sat down. "The gunman has been identified."

Rachael sat down across from her. "That's great news," she said, relieved.

"I said identified, not apprehended."

Rachael's expression visibly changed.

"We were able to lift prints from the stolen car he drove."

"He stole a car?"

"It was parked in the back of your building."

"I see," she said, wondering where the conversation was headed.

"It's curious that the man was from New Jersey."

Rachael frowned. "I wonder what he was doing in Erie?"

"That's what I'm wondering." The detective was quiet for a moment.

Rachael was on pins and needles and afraid her face would show that she was a bundle of nerves.

Finally, the detective said, "Seems you're from New Jersey too."

"Well," she hesitated, then decided that it would be in her best interest to truthfully answer the detective. "I've lived in New Jersey and New York state." Rachael suspected the detective already knew most of her life story by searching public records.

"Your most recent New Jersey address is in Atlantic City, where your boyfriend Ray Russo has the same address."

"Ex-fiancé," Rachael corrected. "May I ask how that is relevant to what happened last night?"

"Just curious why a man from New Jersey was in your building last evening. Of the many buildings, houses, apartments, mobile homes in Erie, why would a man from Atlantic City break into yours?"

Rachael shook her head nervously. "I don't know."

The detective studied Rachael's face, then asked, "The man's name is Mark Bruno, but friends call him Marko. Have you ever heard of him?"

"No, why should I?" Rachael asked, a little too abruptly.

"In your job as a casino bookkeeper, you never ran across a man by this name?"

Rachael was surprised the detective knew of her former job, but didn't ask how she knew. Instead, she simply answered, "No."

"What about Ray Russo? Is there any connection between the two men?"

"I wouldn't have a clue."

The detective fired off a torrent of questions. "Were you having an affair with Marko? Did you break it off with him? Was he angry? Did Ray find out? Is that why you moved here to get away from Marko or Ray or the both of them?"

"How can I have an affair with someone I don't even know? Like I told you, I don't know who Marko is. I've never seen him before. Ever," she emphasized.

"Marko Bruno is a very dangerous man. He has a criminal record a mile-long," the detective said, then changed tactics, "Marko searched your building. We know that because we were able to lift several more fingerprints. He was looking for something. What do you think he was searching for?"

Worn down from the volley of questions, Rachael shook her head and shrugged her shoulders.

Detective Martin rose, picked up her laptop, and walked to the door. "That's all the questions I have for you now. Will you be staying at the hotel while the team processes the scene?"

"Actually, I won't be," she started to explain. "I have to find another place. The hotel doesn't allow pets."

"You have pets? Where? At the storefront? What kind of pets? Are they hiding somewhere? No one has mentioned finding animals. Should I alert them to be on the lookout?"

"No, that won't be necessary. I have a new kitten. She's at the vet—"

The detective interrupted, "New kitten? Wasn't that convenient to have your cat at the vet while a man, who you claim you don't know, broke in your place?"

"My kitten was spayed yesterday. What are you implying?"

"Simple question. Just doing my job. When you check out of the hotel, where are you going to be staying?"

"Honestly, I don't know. I won't be able to search for a new place without my laptop. Is there any way you can retrieve it for me?"

"I'm sorry, no. One of our computer techs is examining it—"

"Examining it? Why?"

"I really don't know his job, like he probably doesn't know mine," the detective said evasively. "When you find out where you're staying, call me."

"I will. And before you leave, how did you know I was staying here?"

"Word travels fast in a small town. I heard it at the diner getting coffee. I'll be in touch," the detective said, leaving.

Rachael rose from her chair and quickly shut the door. She then sat on the bed and covered her face with her hands. *What am I going to do? The mob sent Marko to shoot me and instead those innocent police officers were shot. Will Marko come back and finish the job? Or Ray?*

Why didn't I mail that damn flash drive to Ray when I had the chance in New York?

Rachael's inner voice said, *as long as you have it, you're safe. Give it up, then you won't have something to bargain with. Do you want to end up dead?*

Rachael wanted to cry, but forced back the tears.

A few minutes later, another knock sounded on the door.

Rachael took a deep breath. "Act happy," she said, then opened the door.

It was Stevie.

"Hey, good lookin'," he said with a wink. "Ready to help this poor ole boy git some food?"

Rachael wrinkled her nose in an affectionate manner. "You're a sight for poor eyes. Wait. Did you just say "git"?"

"Hell yes, sugar. That's the language I speak. When I'm relaxed, that's the way I talk."

"Okay, it's kind of cool," she laughed.

"Oh, I'm sorry. Are you ready?" he pronounced in perfect English without a trace of accent.

"I will be in a second. Let me make sure I didn't leave anything behind. I have to check out."

"Why? Did the detective call and give the all clear?"

"She didn't call, but she came to see me."

"When?"

"Just now. Didn't you see her on your way up?"

"No. What did she want?"

"She asked me more questions, which I'd already answered last night." Rachael deliberately didn't tell Stevie about Marko Bruno. "I can't stay here."

"Why?"

"The hotel doesn't allow cats."

"But they have mousers in the back."

"Yeah, in the loading dock. I was told that cats are not permitted in the rooms."

"Well, I can solve that problem. My offer for you to stay at my place still stands."

"I think I'll take you up on it. Thank you so much."

Stevie grabbed Rachael and kissed her on the forehead. "No problem."

Rachael gently broke away. "After we've had breakfast, can you run me by the dollar store? I need to buy some things to tide me over until I can go back home."

"Sure."

"Then we can pick up Intruder," she said, clapping her hands.

"Yes, ma'am." Stevie smiled and held open the door.

Rachael's inner voice said, *Good choice. You'll be close to Katherine's house. Maybe you'll find a way to look for something in pink.*

Rachael thought, *That's my plan.*

Chapter Twenty

In Atlantic City, seven hundred sixty miles from Erie, Ray Russo was getting into his black Dodge Charger. The mob boss wanted him to fly into Indy and steal a car from the long-term parking lot, but Ray declined. He boldly told the boss that he was going on his own terms and to butt out. The boss wasn't happy with that and appealed to Marcel, who ended up agreeing with Ray. The boss backed down and said that Marcel would call the shots. After all, Marcel was the person essential to the financial success of their operation, which was raking in big bucks for a lot of people. However, the boss insisted that Ray arm himself. Since Ray didn't own a handgun, the boss made sure one of his guys gave him one before he left.

Ray reluctantly took the gun. He didn't see a reason to carry an unlicensed gun in the first place. During the long drive to Indiana, a cop could pull him over and search his vehicle. If he lost his temper, which seemed pretty likely — he hated cops — he'd be in big trouble when the cop found an unregistered handgun. Then he'd be busted. Busted meant jail. Jail meant not getting back the flash drive so that Marcel and the mob boss would get off his back.

He had no intention of harming Emma. He just wanted to show her who was boss. His plan was to find her, rough her up a little bit, get the ledger, and head back to Atlantic City. He felt a slight pang of remorse that he'd treated her so badly in the past, and even though it was hard for him to admit it, he missed her. He thought, *Miss her, yes. Love her, no.*

Because Marko had failed to win the prize, Ray decided to go to Erie and keep a low profile. He didn't want to attract the attention of law enforcement, because he wasn't completely positive that Emma hadn't already given the flash drive to the cops. For that reason, he didn't reserve a room in a hotel in the area, but chose a motel in the closest city. He'd use that as a base for his plan, which he called Operation Get It Back.

Chapter Twenty-One

Stevie and Rachael picked up Intruder before the vet clinic closed for the weekend. The kitten was so thrilled to see them and was all purrs and kisses. They drove straight to the Foursquare.

Salina stood waiting on the front porch. Her arms were crossed in a defensive manner and she had a sullen look on her face. She wasn't happy with the new arrangement, or the list of chores she had to do to make the second-story guest room accommodate a woman and her cat, which meant fresh sheets on the bed, then multiple trips up and down the stairs to haul up litterbox, water and food bowls. "Fill the box with kitty litter and put a chocolate on her pillow," Salina groused. "Litter in the box. Check. Chocolate. Nope, I'm not running a four-star hotel."

Locked up in Salina's bedroom was a very unhappy gray cat. Wolfy Joe was used to the run of the house, but Salina thought she should confine him in her room while Rachael, Emma, or what's her name, stayed. He howled like his wolf namesake, but finally quieted down.

As soon as Salina learned Rachael was staying with them for up to two weeks, she texted Katherine. *"Dad is bringing that woman over to stay."*

Katz read the message and texted back, *"You mean Rachael?"*

"When they show up, I think I'll meet them at the door and call her Emma. I'm sure Dad doesn't know that's her real name."

"Not a good idea, Salina. Make the best of it, and Rachael will be gone in no time."

Salina texted a sad face.

Katherine didn't answer.

Getting out of the truck, Rachael could read Salina's hateful expression. So did Stevie. He wasn't happy with his daughter.

While Stevie grabbed two bags of clothing purchases from the back of his truck, Rachael, holding Intruder, stepped back to talk to him. "I really don't want to interfere with how you discipline your daughter, but I think she's served her sentence. Why don't you let her go to the slumber party?"

"Yeah, I think I better, if I'm ever to see my girl smile again."

"Okay, you go give her the good news, and I'll wait a few minutes before I come in. I'll take this time to call Detective Martin and tell her I'm staying with you."

Stevie nodded and walked up to the door, which Salina held wide open. She stuck out her lower lip, but didn't say anything.

"Baby Cake, is it too late for you to call your friend and say you're coming to the party?"

"Oh, Dad!" Salina threw her arms around him. "I love you so much." Then she flew into the house.

"Where are you going? Aren't you going to greet our guest?"

"Just a minute. I have to call Shelly to see if her Mom can take both of us."

Stevie walked outside. "Come in, before you melt out here."

Rachael smiled. She cradled Intruder like a newborn. The kitten was on her back and making kneading-dough movements with her tiny paws.

"Would you like the grand tour?" Stevie asked.

"Yes, I would. I love your house. I love the mission-style furniture. Did you buy it already remodeled?"

"It was ready to move in. Margie Cokenberger's construction crew fixed it up."

"She's really good. I've been pleased with what she's done to the storefront," she said, then bit her lip. She really didn't want to talk about that topic, so she dropped it. "Your kitchen is very modern. I like that, too."

"Well, that's about it for the first floor, unless you want to see the basement. Not much down there."

"Nope, that's okay," she said with a smile. "I think I need to get Intruder to her room." The kitten was squirming to get down.

"Follow me. I'll show you."

On the second-story landing, Stevie pointed, "On the left is my room. Across the hall, two doors down, is Salina's room."

A cat howled behind Salina's closed door.

"Is that Wolfy Joe?" Rachael asked.

"Yep. Do you want me to let him out and meet Intruder?"

"I don't think the two of them should meet right away. Intruder just had an operation and I'm sure she needs to convalesce a bit before we introduce the two of them."

"Okay, but I hope Wolfy Joe doesn't howl all night."

"You could always let him sleep with you," Rachael suggested.

"That ain't happening," Stevie said. "Last time I tried that Wolfy jumped on my face a couple of times, then he got evicted."

Rachael giggled, then asked, "Where's my room?"

"Back here." He led the way down a narrow hall. He pointed out the full bathroom, then opened the door to the guest room. Salina had done a good job getting it ready.

Rachael praised, "Salina did good. I have everything I need, from bath towels to kitten things. I'll thank her later."

"Here's a charging cord for your phone." Stevie was happy his daughter had thought of that.

"You read my mind. I should probably charge my phone before I do anything else."

"Okay, make yourself at home. I'll get the rest of your stuff."

Rachael walked over and hugged him. "Thank you for everything."

"My pleasure."

When Stevie left, Rachael gently placed Intruder on the carpeted floor. She used one of the towels as a cozy bed and put it in the corner. She didn't think Intruder should be jumping up on the bed with her stitches in. The vet had said to keep her quiet for a few days.

By the time Stevie returned with the remaining bags, Intruder was curled up asleep on her new cozy bed.

"She's really tired," Rachael said.

"She must be to pass out like that." Stevie set the bags on the bed. "I have to leave for a few hours. I told my brother Dave I'd help him with something."

"Sure. I have lots to do."

"And what exactly does *lots to do* mean?"

"Girly things. Wash my hair; there wasn't shampoo in my room at the hotel. Put on my face. Try on my new clothes. Stuff like that."

"Have fun with that," he said, starting to leave.

"Oh, wait. Do you have Katz's cell number?"

"Katz?" he asked, wondering why Rachael would want to call Katz.

Rachael explained, "I was going to see if she had an extra laptop sitting around. I need to borrow one while I wait for the cops to give mine back."

"You can use Salina's computer."

"Oh, no. I'd much rather have my own, but thanks."

"Hand me your phone. I'll put Katz's number in your contact's list."

Rachael reached in her purse and pulled her cell out.

When Stevie finished keying in Katherine's number, he handed the phone back to Rachael. "See ya!" he said, leaving. "Try to stay out of trouble."

"I'll try," she winked, then wondered why he knew Katherine's phone number by heart.

She called Katherine right away.

Katherine didn't recognize the number, but answered any way.

"Hi, Katz, this is Rachael Thomas. We met the other day. How are you?"

"I'm fine. I'm so sorry about what happened at your storefront last night."

"I learned this morning that the chief and the other officer are going to be okay."

"Yes, we are very much relieved. What can I help you with?"

"I need to ask a favor. Seems I need a laptop. Mine is back at the storefront." Rachael left out the details about the police holding it. "I was wondering if you had a spare laptop lying around that I could borrow. Stevie mentioned you taught computer classes. I thought you'd have an extra one."

"Yes, I do. Should I bring it next door?"

"How'd you know I was next door?"

Katherine laughed. "Because Salina told me you were coming."

"Oh, she did?" Rachael asked. "Was that before or after Stevie said she could go to the party?"

"She texted me twice."

"I can come over and get it."

"Give me a few hours. Hey, I could give it to you tonight. If Stevie and you don't have plans for dinner, you could come over and have pizza with Jake and me."

"That would be great. I'll have to clear it with Stevie. He's not at home right now."

"How about you come over at seven?"

"Yes, that sounds amazing. I'm sure Stevie will say yes. I'll text, if he doesn't. Oh, and thanks, Katz. Tell the kitties I'm coming over."

"I will."

Rachael ended the call and whispered, "Yay! Perfect! Perfect! Now, I need to figure out how I'm going to search that chair without getting caught."

Good luck with that, her inner voice said.

* * *

Stevie drove into the near-empty parking lot of the Dew Drop Inn, owned by his brother, Dave Sanders, who had inherited the tavern from their late father, Sam. At this time of day, there were few patrons. Stevie spotted his brother's new Highlander and parked next to it. Walking inside the bar, his eyes adjusted to the dimly lit interior.

Eddie the bartender was hand-toweling beer mugs. "Lookin' for your brother?" he asked.

"Yep."

"He's in there," Eddie said, nodding his head in the direction of the room that was a combination store room and office. "Can I git you anything?" he asked.

"Nope, but thanks."

The door was open, so Stevie walked in. He smiled at his brother, who was sitting with his feet up on the desk, and simultaneously sorting through what looked to be bills.

"Hey," Stevie said.

"Come in," Dave said. "Sit yourself down. Want a beer?"

"I'm good. Sorry I haven't been in for a while. I've been really busy with my business."

"Ah, yeah, your business," Dave said, winking. "I've heard she's quite the looker."

Stevie flashed a smile. "Pretty and smart. Her name is Rachael. She owns the storefront next to the hotel."

"Yep, heard that, too."

"Word travels fast. As a matter-of-fact, I'm here to talk about Rachael. I've fallen hard and fast."

"Never heard you say that before. Whatever happened to love 'em and leave 'em? When's the wedding?"

"Could happen, if she'd have me, but until that time, I need to keep Rachael and Salina safe."

"And why come to me?" Dave said, moving his legs from the desk and sitting up normally in his chair.

"Since Dad died, I know you've taken over some of his operations."

"Yeah, what's your point?"

"Since you're still in the loop of what dear old Dad called the family business, and I'm not—"

"Because you went clean and *have* stayed clean. I'm proud of you, bro," Dave said genuinely. "So, what is it you want me to do?"

"We need protection."

"That's easy enough. From whom?"

"The mob."

Dave choked on his own saliva. "The mob? You don't ask for much. How the hell did you get involved with the mob?"

"I'm not, but Rachael's ex-fiancé is connected to one in New Jersey."

"Damn. Tell me more."

"She left him, and came to Erie to open a café."

"Now that's a story. Leave the big city for our little town."

Stevie filled Dave in on the details about Rachael and her fiancé — as much as he knew. "I think he abused her, and she was strong enough to get away from him. Now, she's terrified he's going to find her and kill her."

"Why would he do that?"

"He said he would, and she takes him at his word."

"Does this have something to do with the shooting at her place?"

"Yep. I think the hitman was gunning for her and the cops got in the way."

"What?" Dave asked dubiously. "The mob doesn't hire a hitman to do away with girlfriends that have annoyed their boyfriends. There has to be another reason. Maybe she stole something from them? Money? Drugs?"

"I know it's not drugs. She's definitely not a drug user. Maybe money. I don't know what. However, I do intend to find out."

"Out of curiosity, where was Rachael when the cops were shot?"

"She was with me. We had a date. I took her home and all hell broke loose."

"Where's she now?"

"She's staying with Salina and me until the cops say she can move back to her place. I don't want this gangster anywhere near my home, with Rachael and my daughter there."

"Understood. This can be arranged. I can have my guys keep an eye out on your house, but once she goes back to her place, that'll be difficult."

"Yeah, I know. You don't want to call attention to yourself. I get it."

"Rachael lives on the main drag. Those old biddies in the neighborhood watch group don't miss a trick."

"Yep, I hear ya." Stevie didn't mention how Gladys Kramer was one of those biddies and the one who called in the break in.

"How long will Rachael be at your house?"

"Up to two weeks."

"Okay. I'll take care of it," Dave said.

"I appreciate it, but there's one more favor I need to ask."

"What? Name it."

"Text me if a guy comes in the bar and appears to be from out-of-town, especially if he asks a bunch of questions about Rachael or me."

"I can do that too. Does this dude have a name?"

"Ray Russo. He's Sicilian."

"Yeah, right, little brother, like the *Godfather*?"

"Just sayin'."

"Okay, if I see a Sicilian, I'll text."

"Okay." Stevie started to get up.

"Do you know what he looks like?"

"Nope."

"Then how will I know he's Sicilian?"

"Don't know, but I trust you'll figure it out."

Dave chuckled. "I reckon I can do that. Take care now."

"Thanks," Stevie said, leaving.

* * *

Later, at seven p.m., Stevie and Rachael walked over to the pink mansion.

Jake answered the door. "Hey, long time no see," he said to Stevie, then glanced at Rachael. "You must be Rachael. I'm Jake. Katz's other half. Come right in."

Katherine stood in the living room's doorway. "Hello. I'm so glad you two made it. Let's sit in here."

Stevie and Rachael walked in and sat down on a damask-covered loveseat while Katherine moved to a vintage wingback chair.

Rachael wondered if that was the old chair Salina had talked about.

Jake stood at the door. "I'll be back in a minute. Got to pick up the pizzas."

Stevie rose from the loveseat. "Hey, I'll come with."

"Perfect, because I wanted to ask you something about my Jeep. Sometimes it makes this funny noise . . . ." His voice trailed off as Stevie and he left the house.

Katherine asked Rachael, "Are you getting settled at Stevie's?"

"I'm so thankful he offered me a room to stay. I was at the Erie Hotel, but when they found out I was picking up my kitten, the woman at the front desk said the hotel didn't allow pets."

"I think that's a ridiculous policy. How is your kitten? I've forgotten what you named her."

"Intruder. She's fine, but very tired from the spay."

"She'll be climbing the curtains in no time," Katherine joked. "I found a spare laptop. It's in my basement classroom. I'll go get it."

Rachael didn't offer to go with her. "Oh, thanks, that's great."

As soon as Katherine left the room, Rachael got down on her hands and knees and began feeling underneath the cushion of the second wingback chair, then she checked the lining. It was intact, so she crawled over to the chair Katherine had just vacated and glanced underneath it. She found the torn opening. "Eureka," she whispered. She ran her hand inside, but was disappointed she didn't find the flash drive. She tipped the chair and moved her hand inside a second time. Still nothing. She righted the chair just as Katherine walked in.

"Did you lose something?" she asked.

"Oh, yes," Rachael said, startled. "My hair barrette. It's made of glass."

"I'll be on the lookout for it. What color is it?"

"Pink," Rachael stuttered. "Pink glass."

"Maybe it fell in the yard when you came over," Katherine suggested, wondering why Rachael was down on all fours looking in the vicinity of the famous chair. Something set off faint alarm bells, but she couldn't quite pinpoint the suspicion.

"Hope so. It was a gift," Rachael said, spinning the yarn as she spoke. "I'll look when I go home."

"It'll be dark. Better use a flashlight."

"I'll use the one on my cell phone." Rachael rose and sat back on the loveseat.

Katherine moved over and handed her the laptop. "Keep it as long as you need it."

"Thanks so much."

"I ran a check on it to make sure it didn't have a computer virus, so you don't have to worry about that."

"That's good to know." Rachael leaned down and placed the laptop on the floor next to her satchel purse. Then she looked around the room. "Where are the cats?"

"I locked them in their playroom."

"Locked?" Rachael asked.

"I have an outside lock on the door because Scout, my resident Houdini cat, opens doors."

Rachael giggled. "Cadabra learned that trick from Roy. He was Magic Harry's animal trainer." Then as soon as she said it, she immediately changed the subject, "Oh, I was looking forward to seeing all your cats."

Katherine hesitated before answering. She didn't want to let Scout and Abra out because their last encounter with Rachael had totally stressed Abra out. She'd really preferred, and Jake agreed, that the Siamese never see Rachael again. Finally, Katherine spoke, "I'll see if they want to come down. Give me a minute and I'll be right back." Katherine left the room and bound up the stairs. She opened the door to the playroom. Five cats were curled up in their cozy beds, except for Iris and Abby. They shot out of the room and ran down the stairs.

Katherine glanced over at the cozy bed Scout and Abra were in. In a split second, they had gone from being fast asleep to sitting up, wide-eyed awake, as if they would run out as well.

"No, my girls. Go back to sleep."

Their ears perked up in interest, then they laid back down.

Iris and Abby, partners in crime, raced into the living room. They homed in on the wingback chair. They knew someone had been messing with it, but the scent wasn't their humans'. It had to be that other woman who smelled like the pink prize. Their ears swiveled back, then forward. They looked at each other, and then Iris dove through the torn lining.

Katherine returned to the room. "Iris, you silly girl, get out of my chair."

"Yowl," Iris sassed.

Rachael laughed. "Why does she like your chair?"

Katherine proceeded to tell the "feline loot hidden in the chair" story.

Rachael acted like she'd never heard it before. "Oh, that's so cute."

"As soon as Jake and Stevie get back, I'll have to put them up."

"Why? They're not bothering me."

"Because they'll steal the pizza right off your plate."

Rachael laughed again and hoped it didn't sound too forced. She was upset she didn't find the flash drive and wondered where it was.

While Katherine and Rachael continued to chat, Abby had something else in mind. She trotted over to the blue-and-white-patterned oriental bowl, on the floor next to the fireplace, and fished out a pink flash drive. She clenched it in her jaws. When she let go, it dropped to the wood floor and made a sound. But the humans were too engaged in their conversation to notice. To guard her treasure, she placed her right paw on top of it and stayed in that position, like an Egyptian Bastet statue, and didn't move until Jake and Stevie returned. Then she pushed it with her paw behind the bowl. "Chirp," she cried happily.

Jake and Stevie came back and entered the room with two large pizza boxes. "Let's eat in the kitchen," he said.

Katherine added, "It's a cat-free zone."

Iris yowled in protest. Abby didn't care. She'd already secured her loot.

Jake led the way. Stevie and Rachael followed.

Katherine remained behind, "Come on Iris and Abby. Let's put you back in the playroom."

The cats didn't budge.

"Treat?"

Iris became very vocal while Abby spoke in her much more subdued voice.

Katherine enticed the cats upstairs to the playroom by saying "treat, treat, and more treats." Then she locked them in the room. The cats protested loudly on the other side of the door.

"I know, my treasures. It was a dirty trick. I'll give you treats later."

Chapter Twenty-Two

A Week Later at the Pink Mansion

Katherine stepped through her front doorway to check for the morning mail. She was barefoot, and had planned to rush out, grab the mail, and run back inside. The Victorian-style mailbox was empty, so she turned to go back in, but something unusual caught her eye next door. She glanced over at the Foursquare. Stevie's truck was gone. Nothing extraordinary about that; she assumed he was at work. Then she saw Rachael's Tercel parked in front. She hadn't seen it parked there before. She remembered it from the first time Rachael visited her.

She hadn't seen Stevie or Rachael since they had come over for pizza, but Salina was keeping her updated on what they'd been doing. As Salina put it, Stevie and Rachael were "hanging out," leaving the teen stuck at home, frantically texting her friends to complain.

As Katherine moved to go back inside, Rachael walked out and headed toward her car. She was carrying her black kitten, Intruder.

"Hi, Rachael," Katherine greeted.

"Oh, hello, Katz. I just got word that I can move back into my place. Isn't that amazing?"

Katherine joined Rachael on the sidewalk. She tiptoed to avoid stepping on something sharp. "That's such good news. Can I help you carry anything?"

"Thanks, but I really don't have much."

"So, this is the little girl? Can I hold her?"

"Yes, please do. Do you mind if I go back inside and get my last remaining bags?"

"Sure."

Rachael handed Katherine the kitten and walked back into the Foursquare.

Katherine held the kitten against her chest and kissed her gently on the top of the head. The kitten purred. "You really have a loud purr, little one," Katherine cooed. "I haven't held a kitten in a very long time."

The black cat mewed, and ran her pink tongue over her lips, then reared up and licked Katherine on the nose.

"Thank you for the kiss. I think I love you!"

Rachael returned and placed her remaining bags on the floorboard behind the driver's side, then took Intruder from Katherine. She put the kitten inside a small cat carrier on the back seat. She shut the car door and faced Katherine. "I'm so relieved I can move back."

"I bet you are."

"Actually, I could have moved back yesterday, but I had to hire a cleaning crew to clean." Rachael didn't mention that they were a special cleaning service that dealt with crime scenes.

Katherine understood what Rachael hadn't said. She had to do the same thing several years before, when Patricia Marston shot Jake in the pink mansion's living room. She launched into another topic, "I looked and looked for your barrette, but I didn't find it."

"Barrette?" Rachael questioned.

"Yeah, the pink glass one you lost."

"Oh, that one. You know, with everything that's going on, I'd totally forgotten about it."

"Well, okay. I won't keep you. I know you're anxious to go back home and get this little one out of this heat."

"I'll drop off your laptop as soon as I can."

"No worries. Keep it as long as you want."

"Super." Rachael climbed in her car and drove off.

Katherine headed back home to see Scout and Abra doing their meerkat pose on the windowsill of the first-floor turret window. She could tell they were crying their Siamese lungs out.

"Oh, great. Now what?" Usually when Scout and Abra did their loud caterwauls, they were tattling on the other cats.

She rushed in the house to find a white blizzard of pulverized facial tissue. A trail of shredded tissue led from the front door to the living room.

"Darn it, you guys. Which one of you did it?" she accused.

Iris trotted over and yowled. She almost sounded embarrassed.

"Miss Siam, you don't have to plead guilty to everything. I know this wasn't you."

Scout and Abra jumped down and fled the scene. Katherine called after them, "Thanks for helping me clean up this mess."

Katherine thought, *this is the handiwork of Dewey and Crowie. Their claws are as sharp as razors and more efficient than a paper shredder.*

The guilty seal-point brothers wrestled in a fluffy tissue mound near the credenza.

Abby became very vocal, which was unusual for the Abyssinian. "Chirp! Chirp!" she cried in her soft voice.

Nearby, Lilac sneezed. Katherine picked her up and wiped the shred of tissue stuck on her nose. She set her down next to Abby.

Heading over to Dewey and Crowie, she tripped over the empty tissue box, but caught herself before she fell. The movement scared the cats who scattered to the four corners of the room. Reaching down to pick up the tissue, she noticed a pink object in the middle of the pile. "There you are," she said, thinking she had just found Rachael's missing barrette. When she brought it closer to her face, she saw that it was a USB flash drive.

It was unlike any flash drive she'd ever seen. The memory sticks she used were black with a sliding red button. This one was a two-piece with a removable cap.

"I wonder who this belongs to?" she asked. She thought about who had recently been in her house. Through the process of elimination, she checked off who couldn't be the owner. Jake used the same kind of memory stick that she did. Salina didn't use flash drives. Margie and Chief London were ruled out, especially Margie, who resisted the computer like a swarm of bees, and had her daughter pull her emails and print them.

"Let's see," she thought aloud. "Stevie and Rachael were here. Stevie is like Margie and doesn't like computers."

The hairs on Katherine's neck rose. "Rachael! The pink barrette! Well, it does look like the front of a glass barrette, that is, if you don't scrutinize it, but why did she lie? Why couldn't she just ask if I'd found a pink flash drive?"

Abby rubbed against Katherine's legs and reached up to be held. Katherine glanced down at the Abyssinian.

"Chirp!" Abby cried.

"No, sweetie. Mommy's thinking."

Katherine began to put two and two together, literally, the thief and the thief's accomplice. "Iris stole it. Abby took it from Iris. Dewey and Crowie thought it was a toy."

Holding the flash drive, Katherine walked downstairs to her basement-level computer classroom. She inserted the drive in a laptop and did a malware and virus check. When the drive passed the tests, Katherine removed it from the port and took it over to her computer. She plugged it in.

Reading the directory, she noticed there were Excel files as well as PDF files. First, she pulled up one of the Excel files and found it was a list of bank accounts at a number of banks. The font was very small so she enlarged it and realized the spreadsheet included routing numbers for international banks. She was surprised that none of these banks were based in the U.S.

She said aloud, "Why would Rachael have this?"

Second, Katherine closed out the spreadsheet and retrieved a PDF file. The file appeared to be some kind of accounting — a ledger, perhaps — of names, addresses, banks, and business enterprises. Out of curiosity, she wrote down several of the names, then did a Google search on each person. Each name was a known criminal who had a long list of infractions, ranging from embezzlement to fraud to money laundering. Of the five names she researched, only one man didn't produce any hits.

Katherine's gut-instinct told her that Rachael — somehow — had taken the flash drive and moved to Erie to get away from someone. Maybe the man who shot Chief London was gunning for Rachael? Maybe he was a disgruntled boyfriend or husband? Or, perhaps, Rachael was a felon running from the law? The hitman, or whoever he was — bad man —might be coming back to get the flash drive. Rachael doesn't have it and is desperate to get it back.

Katherine said, frustrated, "She doesn't have a clue that one of my cats stole it out of her purse, or does she? Why else would she be searching for a missing barrette in the vicinity of the infamous wingback chair? Maybe Salina told her about some of my cats' antics?"

Then Katherine shuddered with fear. *The entire time Rachael stayed with Stevie and Salina, the gunman could have returned and shot every one of them until he got back what he wanted. It would be my history repeating itself — a recurrence of when my New York school friend visited and brought the Russian mob to my door in search of a valuable diamond*, she thought.

Katherine tugged her phone out of her back pocket and called Detective Martin.

The detective answered happily, "Hi, Katz. So good to hear from you."

"Oh, gosh, Linda, I really need to talk to you. I think I have information that may help solve why Chief London and Officer Troy were shot."

"Start from the beginning?"

"I found a pink USB flash drive in my house. I plugged it into a non-network computer in case there was something bad on it. Well, what I discovered was a different kind of bad. I need you to come over as soon as possible."

"Sure, but can you give me a little bit more information. Do you know who it belongs to?"

"I'm ninety-nine percent sure it belongs to Rachael Thomas."

"Rachael Thomas? How do you know her?"

"She's been to my home on two different occasions." Katherine proceeded to fill the detective in on the particulars of who, what, when and where. She began with her coincidental meeting with Rachael, who once worked as a cat wrangler for Harry DeSutter, the famous magician. "Stevie Sanders suggested to Rachael that she visit me and ask about volunteering at the rescue center. When she saw Scout and Abra, there was a tearful reunion. Unknown to Rachael, Salina, Stevie's daughter, videoed the event and uploaded it to YouTube. The video went viral and made national news."

"Wow! What a coincidence."

"A few days later, a gunman broke into Rachael's storefront and shot Chief London and Officer Troy. I think he'd been looking for Rachael and didn't know where she was until he watched the video on YouTube or the news. He was gunning for Rachael."

"So, the chief and Officer Troy were at the wrong place at the wrong time."

"Yes, and the gunman broke into Rachael's place to find the flash drive."

"Ms. Thomas must have been carrying it in her purse or pocket."

"But Rachael didn't have it because one of my cats stole it out of her purse. It's been at the pink mansion since she first visited me."

The detective snickered, "Don't tell me. Abby, right?"

"Possibly, but there's lots more. When Rachael came to my home a second time, I caught her searching the wingback chair where the cats hide their loot. She said she was looking for a pink barrette—"

"But was really looking for the flash drive," the detective finished. "Have you read any of the files that are on it?"

"Yes, and you need to see them."

The detective said excitedly, "Okay, this is big. I'll be there in five minutes." She hung up.

Katherine paced the floor. Conflicting thoughts popped in her head. *Maybe I should confront Rachael with this? Maybe I should tell Stevie about it? If I do tell Stevie, maybe he'll get mad at me for disrespecting his new girlfriend, and never speak to me again?*

Looking through the front door sidelight, she saw an unmarked sedan pull up and park.

Detective Martin got out and hurried to the door. Katherine opened it before she could ring the bell.

"Hello, Katz, before you show me the flash drive, have you told anyone else about this?"

"No, not even Jake. I called you right away."

"For now, please keep this confidential."

"Yes, I promise."

"Lead the way."

"Follow me to my classroom on the lower floor."

The two women didn't speak as they made their way to the basement, then Katherine said, "I don't think Rachael is a criminal. I think she made a bad choice."

"We'll see."

Katherine handed the flash drive to the detective, who inserted it into her laptop.

"I've looked at two of the files: one's a spreadsheet; the other is a PDF file," Katherine began. "The PDF file looks like some sort of ledger. Four out of the five names I Googled are known criminals. Two of them have been indicted in federal court for international money laundering. However, there was one name on my list that didn't come up with any hits. He might be going under an alias."

"What's his name on the ledger?"

"Ray Russo—"

"Did you say Ray Russo?"

"Yes." Katherine looked at the detective curiously.

"Ray Russo was Rachael's fiancé. They lived together for six months in an apartment in Atlantic City. Ray is currently employed by a casino as a security guard. Before Rachael moved to Erie, she was a bookkeeper at this same casino."

"Incredible," Katherine said, shocked. "How in the world does a cat wrangler working for a celebrity like Harry DeSutter end up being a bookkeeper in a casino?"

"I don't have time to talk about everything I know about Ms. Thomas. After Mr. DeSutter fired her—"

"Because Abra was stolen out of her carrier," Katherine finished. "I know all about that."

"Ms. Thomas went to a university to be a vet tech. When that didn't work out, she changed her major to bookkeeping and graduated two years later."

"Is Ray Russo a criminal?"

"Yes, big-time. He's a member of one of New Jersey's most notorious organized crime groups."

"The mob?"

Detective Martin nodded.

"If he's a criminal, why didn't I find anything about him on Google?"

"Because Google has nothing on the FBI's criminal database."

"I'm curious if Rachael used the name Emma in her last job?"

"Why do you ask?"

"Because that was her name when she worked for the magician."

"Emma is her first name; Rachael is her middle name."

Katherine frowned. "I feel like a snitch for pointing the finger at Rachael. Everything I've told you is circumstantial evidence. I didn't see Rachael take the flash drive. I never saw her with it. I didn't see my cats steal it. With my cats and my handling of the flash drive, Rachael's fingerprints probably aren't even on it."

The detective chuckled. "I'm bankin' that Abby's DNA would be on it—"

"And Iris, Dewey and Crowie, and whatever cat of mine played with it."

"Yep."

"If Rachael is guilty of a criminal offense, will I have to testify? I mean, how do I tell the world my cats are thieves?"

"You won't have to. I'm sure you'll be regarded as a good Samaritan for finding the drive and giving it to us."

"In your professional opinion, what's your take on this?"

"Rachael was a bookkeeper. Perhaps, in her job, she came across incriminating computer files. She smelled a rat, made a flash drive copy of the files, and then booked it out of town."

"The plot thickens."

"Indeed, it does." The detective removed the USB flash drive from her laptop. She pulled a clear plastic bag out of her purse, then dropped it in the bag. "Katz, what you've discovered is way over the jurisdiction of the Indiana State Police. I'll upload the contents of this drive to the FBI. In the meantime, be quiet as a mouse. Not a word."

"I promise." Katherine pantomimed the zipping of her lips.

"Okay, show me the way out. Your house is huge. I forgot to leave a trail of bread crumbs when we came down here," the detective said, grinning.

"Oh, you can go out this door. I'm lucky to have a house with a walkout basement."

"Cool. Okay, I'll talk to you soon. Give a hug to the cats, especially my favorite one, Abby."

"Yes, I will."

Detective Martin left and Katherine shut and locked the door behind her.

Chapter Twenty-Three

Rachael Returns to the Storefront

Rachael parked in the storefront's back parking lot and quickly removed the cat carrier off the back seat. She talked quietly to the kitten, who was fast asleep. "Wake up, little one. We're home now. You won't be cooped up in a room again listening to that big, loud gray cat. You'll have the full run of two floors."

"Mew," Intruder cried, waking up.

Rachael inserted the key to her courtyard gate and turned the lock; then she opened her back door. Yesterday, while the professional cleaners worked wonders on the steps and third floor, Stevie changed the locks on three doors.

Walking inside, she set the cat carrier on the kitchen counter and moved to the next room to turn up the air. The place had the fresh scent of cinnamon. Rachael wondered if Intruder would like it.

The kitten sneezed inside her carrier.

Rachael giggled. "I guess not."

Picking up the cat carrier, she climbed two stories and placed Intruder in her bedroom. When Rachael swung open the metal gate, the kitten darted out and raced around the room.

"Everything is ready for you, my darling. I have to go somewhere. I'll see you soon."

Rachael went back to the first-floor kitchen and looked for her laptop. It wasn't there. "Dang, I can't believe the police still have it," she complained.

She returned to the Tercel and made several trips to unload the vehicle. Placing the laptop she'd borrowed from Katherine on the counter, she logged in and checked her new email address. Lawrence, her grandmother's boyfriend, had emailed her earlier that morning. Rachael anxiously opened it and prepared for the worst, but instead the news was good. Her Grammy was comfortably living in an assisted living place on the Upper West Side of Manhattan. Lawrence said she was in good spirits and would have written the message herself, but the arthritis in Pearl's hands was bothering her.

Rachael breathed a sigh of relief. "Good news," she said aloud. "Oh, Grammy, I so much want to talk to you." Rachael answered the email with a smiley face. "I'm fine. I'm happy. I'll call you soon. Love you," she typed.

After sending the email, Rachael reached into one of the cabinet drawers and lifted out a new burner phone. She removed it from the packaging and threw the phone into her purse. She had a very important call to make, but didn't want to make it in the storefront. She suspected the police had bugged her place. She also thought that if she asked Stevie to look for surveillance stuff, that would raise a red flag. She didn't want to confess to her boyfriend that she'd stolen something from the mob.

She headed back outside, locked the door, and went to her car. She drove out of town several miles, and pulled off the highway to a secluded parking area at the entrance of a walking trail. She took a deep breath, and punched in Ray Russo's number.

It rang twice, then a familiar voice answered.

Not recognizing the phone number on his screen, Ray answered in a gruff voice. "This better not be a damn robocall."

"No, Ray, it's me."

"It's about time you called, Emma," Ray said, enunciating her name in an irritated voice.

"I need to talk to you," Rachael said.

"I imagine you do."

"I have made a new life for myself. I just want to be left alone. I need you to call off your boss from sending another hitman to kill me."

"Then give me what I want?"

"I lost it."

Ray burst out laughing. "Good one, Emma, you never were good at lying."

Rachael paused, thought hard about what she was going to say, then spoke, "Hear me out."

"I'm all ears."

"I didn't take the flash drive intentionally. I didn't know what was on it. It was pink so I assumed it was some kind of photo backup. I mean, what man stores confidential files on a girly flash drive?"

"That's pretty sexist, coming from you, a throwback to the hippie days," he insulted. "Go on. Get to the point."

"By the time I was on my way to my new place—"

Ray interrupted. "Yeah, in some god-forsaken town called Erie in good old boring Indiana. How stupid of you to be on national news," he criticized.

"Didn't take you long to make fun of me."

"So, spit it out! What do you want to tell me?"

"When I read some of the files, I knew I had to return it to the bank's safe deposit box, but I didn't know how."

"Likely story," he said, disbelieving. "So, did you hand it over to the Feds?"

"Absolutely not."

"What about the police? Did you give it to them after Marko shot the two cops?"

"How do you know that?"

"About Marko? Or the cops?" he asked sarcastically.

"What do you mean?"

"Well, for your information, Marko is dead. He sleeps with the fishes. And your casino coworker, Rose, the fat old hag, she's dead, too."

"Rose? Oh, no. You didn't kill Rose, did you?"

"My hands are clean."

"I hate you," Rachael screamed. "Why would you kill an innocent person?"

"I assume you're talking about Rose, and not poor Marko."

Rachael tried to calm down, but wanted to reach through the phone and strangle the monster. Finally, she said, "Where do we go from here?"

"You'll have to find it."

"Then what?"

"Give it to me."

"How will I do that? I'm not coming to Atlantic City."

"We can meet in Erie."

"Never!"

"It won't be inconvenient."

"Why?" she asked in fear of what he might answer.

"Because I'm already in town." Ray disconnected the call.

Rachael panicked. *What do I do? I have to get out of here*, she thought.

A black Dodge Charger pulled up and parked beside her. It looked like the same make and model Ray drove. Terrified, she looked over at the car, thinking it was Ray, but she couldn't see through the tinted glass. She nervously started the engine but was relieved when a husband and wife got out with their two dogs. The husband smiled.

Rachael waved, then reached in her purse and removed Detective Martin's card. Using the same burner phone she'd used to call Ray, she punched in the detective's number; her call went directly to voice mail. She hurriedly left a message, "This is Rachael Thomas. I need to talk to you ASAP. Please call me at this number." She hung up, put the Tercel in gear, then drove to the place Stevie told her to go if she needed help — the Dew Drop Inn.

On the drive there, she kept checking her rearview mirror to see if anyone was following her. Assured that she wasn't, she drove into the bar's parking lot and parked in the back. Before she went inside, she texted Stevie and told him she needed help and was at the Dew Drop Inn. Stevie texted back immediately and said he'd meet her there as soon as he could.

By the time Rachael walked into the bar, Stevie had already contacted his brother, Dave, who was waiting for her at the door. He quickly ushered her to his office, but before he shut the door, he directed several men sitting at a front table to stand outside and guard the building.

Stepping into the room, Dave asked, "Rachael, I presume? What's up?"

Rachael dropped into the closest chair and gave a complete account of Ray Russo being in Erie. She left out the part about why he was in town.

"Just relax," Dave said, leaving. "Stevie's on his way."

"Thank you," she said.

A few minutes went by, then Rachael's cell rang. It was Detective Martin. "Hello," Rachael answered. "I need to urgently speak to you. My life is in danger."

The detective played it cool, not revealing the fact she knew quite a bit about Ms. Thomas and wouldn't be surprised that her call had something to do with the flash drive. "I can meet you at the police department?"

"Oh, no, I can't drive anywhere."

"Okay, then, where can we talk?"

"I'm at the Dew Drop Inn."

"Dew Drop Inn? Why are you there?"

"My boyfriend, Stevie Sanders, told me to come here if I needed help."

"Okay, I can be there in approximately ten minutes." The detective hung up.

When Dave came back to check on Rachael, she told him the detective was coming.

"Thanks for the warning."

"What do you mean?"

"I need to call my boys off. We don't want Detective Martin to get shot." Dave hurriedly left the room.

Rachael sat back and wrung her hands. *What have I gotten into? What kind of people are the Sanders family? What did Dave mean about not wanting the detective to get shot?*

Rachael's phone rang. It was Stevie. "Hey babe, will you be here soon?" she asked worriedly.

"Nope. GPS says I'm sixty minutes away," he said with a serious tone.

"Detective Martin is meeting me here."

"Really? I better call Dave and tell him to warn his boys to not shoot her."

"Why would they shoot her?"

"Because my family is very protective of kin, and my brother swore he'd look out for you."

"Aww, that's sweet, but I think Dave has already told them to stand down."

"What's going on? Why is the detective coming there?"

"Ray's in town."

"How do you know?"

"I called him."

"Why? That makes no sense."

"Stevie, he's in Erie. I'm terrified he's going to hurt me."

"You should be talking to the prosecutor for a restraining order, not the detective. She ain't your friend."

"I need to get something off my chest."

"So, here's the part where you confess to the detective about something you haven't even told me about. Right?"

"I'm sorry, Stevie. So, so sorry."

"Don't say anything incriminating without talking first to a lawyer in private."

"Why would I say anything incriminating?" Rachael asked, wondering why Stevie said that, because she hadn't told him about the flash drive.

"Because I'm an ex-con and I know these things."

"I won't."

"Hang in there," Stevie said icily, hanging up.

Rachael thought, *I would've felt more confident if he'd said he loved me, or cared for me. He's been so buddy-buddy, so why did he just give me the cold shoulder?* "Hang in there," she repeated cynically.

On the way to the Dew Drop Inn, Detective Martin called Chief London, who was back on the job. After she'd left the pink mansion, she'd talked to him about what was going on, what was on the flash drive, and how the New Jersey mob was involved. When she mentioned meeting Rachael at the tavern, he advised her that she should have backup. "That place can be a viper's nest," he warned. The detective declined the offer of assistance.

Finding only a few cars in the bar's parking lot, the detective didn't think it was too much of a viper's nest. She parked and hurried inside.

Dave escorted her to his office, then left the two women alone.

Rachael stood up. "Thank you for coming."

"Can we sit?"

"Yes." Rachael sat down in the chair she'd been sitting on.

Detective Martin sat at the desk, facing the door. "Do you care if I take notes on my laptop?" she asked.

"Sure. No problem."

The detective opened her laptop. "What did you want to talk to me about?"

"Ray Russo, my ex-fiancé, is in town. I talked to him less than an hour ago."

The detective began typing, then asked, "You said you talked to him. Was that in person or on the phone?"

"On my cell."

"So how do you know that Ray is physically in Erie if you didn't talk to him in person?"

"He said he was."

The detective got up. "Excuse me for a minute. I need to make a call." She left the room, called the state police dispatcher to issue an all-points bulletin. "Ray Russo is a criminal person of interest. He may be armed. Use great caution if you find him." She gave the make and model of his vehicle and the New Jersey license plate number she had gathered from researching the FBI's database. "I believe he is in Erie." She ended the call, returned to the room and sat back down.

"Sorry about that," she apologized in a friendly voice. "What else did Ray and you talk about?"

"Ray said Marko Bruno shot the two cops. He said he was a New Jersey mob hitman who screwed up. Ray said I was the target."

"Back at the hotel, you told me you didn't know who Marko was. I assume that wasn't true."

"I didn't know him personally. I just knew him as an associate of Ray's."

"Mob associate?"

"Yes, but he's dead now."

"Dead?"

"The mob had him killed. I don't know the details because Ray didn't tell me."

"So, you're afraid Ray is going to harm you?"

"Why, yes," Rachael said, surprised. "That's why I called you. He's a monster. He said my co-worker at the casino, Rose, was dead. I think he killed her or had her killed."

"What was the motive?"

"I presume he tried to get information from her about my whereabouts and she didn't cooperate."

"Seems like an awful lot of trouble for a guy you only lived with for six months. I think you need to tell me the full story."

Rachael hesitated.

The detective reached into her pocket and lifted out a plastic bag. Inside was the pink flash drive.

Rachael gasped. "Where did you find it?"

"Does this belong to you?"

Rachael didn't answer, but shifted guiltily in her seat.

"I thought so." The detective stood up, tugged a pair of handcuffs from her other pocket, and walked over to Rachael. "Stand up. Emma Rachael Thomas you have the right to remain silent," she began reciting the Miranda warning. "Anything you say can be used against you in a court of law. You have the right to an attorney. If you cannot afford one, the court will appoint one for you."

Rachael started to cry.

"Turn around and bring your arms back so I can cuff you." The detective quickly handcuffed Rachael. "Ms. Thomas, I'm arresting you on suspicion of obstructing justice."

Rachael pleaded, "Please don't arrest me. I'll tell you everything I know."

"Sit back down," the detective said sternly.

Rachael did what she was told. The handcuffs prevented her from sitting comfortably on the chair. She bent her head and sobbed.

The detective took her seat behind the desk and resumed typing. After a few minutes, she looked up at Rachael. "Care to start all over again? Does the flash drive belong to you?"

"No, it belongs to Ray. When I left him, I took it out of our bank's safe deposit box. I didn't know what was on it. When I found out it contained files about the mob, I wanted to return it, but I was afraid Ray would catch me and hurt me. I've racked my brain on what I should do. Then when the officers were shot, I knew the mob was behind it. I was going to call Ray and agree to give it back, but I lost it. I lost the damn thing." Rachael started crying again.

"For starters, you could have turned it over to the FBI."

The detective saved her file and closed her laptop. She called the Erie police dispatcher. "This is Detective Linda Martin. I need backup. I'm at the Dew Drop Inn, in the back office." She ended the call.

"Why do you need backup? I'm not dangerous," Rachael said through tears.

The detective rolled her eyes. "You're not dangerous, but your fiancé is."

"Ex."

"It's a matter of semantics."

Dave barged into the office. "What's going on?" he demanded.

"Mr. Sanders, I need you to step back and leave."

"I have a right to know. You're on my property."

"Now," the detective ordered in a loud voice.

Dave reluctantly left. He walked back to the bar and texted Stevie. *"Bro, that detective woman arrested Rachael. I'm not sure on what charge."*

Stevie texted back. *"Make sure she gets an attorney."*

"How the hell do I do that?" Dave texted back. *"Listen, little brother, I'm done. This woman is way too much trouble."*

Stevie didn't text back.

Chief London and Officer Griswall, a temporary replacement for Officer Troy, arrived in separate vehicles.

Officer Troy was still convalescing and getting rehab for his injuries.

They stepped in and assisted the detective by walking Rachael out of the bar and placing her in the back of the officer's cruiser.

"Officer Griswall, take her to the chief's office and stand guard until we get there," the detective instructed. Then she said to Chief London, "I hope you're up to this."

"A couple of bruised ribs aren't going to keep me from doing my job."

"My FBI contact is meeting us down at the station. He'll talk to Rachael and take her into custody. For her sake, I hope she cooperates."

"Didn't she cooperate with you?" the chief asked.

"I don't trust her. I caught her in several lies."

"What kind of lies were they? 'Cover your tracks' lies or 'lead you the wrong way' lies?"

"Both. In my opinion, if she levels with the FBI, I don't think she'll be prosecuted."

"Doesn't sound as easy as that when you have the mob after you."

"She'll have to testify against them in federal court."

"That's a very risky proposition. The mob will be after her with all guns loaded. What if she doesn't agree?"

"If she doesn't, she'll serve time in prison where the mob will pay another prisoner to kill her. But, if she's smart, she'll become a protected witness until and during the trial, then enter the Witness Protection Program."

"Sounds about right. Poor Mr. Sanders won't be happy about this," the chief commented.

"I agree," she sighed. "I hate to say it, but Stevie really has a hard time keeping women."

"Or, look at it this way, maybe Stevie will go with her."

"I doubt it. He has his daughter to think about."

"Now to settle this mess, we need to find Ray Russo. We don't need a half-cocked gangster in our community."

"I issued an all-points bulletin."

"Yes, I know."

"We'll find him," the detective answered with confidence.

The chief asked, "Are you sure Rachael will testify against him?"

"Oh, yes. Rachael is scared to death of him. She told me earlier that he confessed to murdering her co-worker in Atlantic City. And for the cherry on top of the fudge sundae — drumroll, please — Ray said Mark Bruno was the hitman who shot you and Officer Troy."

"Couldn't make this stuff up. Oh, by the way, where did you find the flash drive? I know as a fact the police combed Rachael's entire storefront. I've read their list of found items. I don't recall seeing a USB flash drive on the list."

The detective chuckled. "Katz Cokenberger found it."

"You're kidding me, right? Where?"

"At the pink mansion."

"What? I didn't know Katz knew Rachael Thomas?"

The detective brought the chief up to date.

The chief grinned. "You don't need to say anything else. I'm banking one of Katz's cats took it out of Rachael's purse or pocket."

"Yes, I suspect an Abyssinian named Abby."

"No, don't think so. Sorry about your police work, detective, but I suspect Iris. She's picked my pocket several times."

The detective laughed, then said, "I'll meet you downtown."

The chief tipped his tasseled hat, got into his vehicle, and drove off. On the way to the police department, he received a call from the dispatcher, his niece, Maureen. "Gladys Kramer reported suspicious activity in front of Rachael Thomas's storefront. A man in a black Dodge Charger, with New Jersey plates, is in a fight with Ted, the bouncer."

"Okay, I'm heading there now," the chief said, turning on his siren. "New Jersey plates. Could be our suspect," he said aloud. He raced to Main Street to find the situation well in hand. Ted, a part-time wedding bouncer and as big as an industrial refrigerator, was holding with one hand a dangling man whose arms were flailing back-and-forth like a rag doll. Standing nearby, Gladys and her husband Al were yelling for help.

"Total mayhem," the chief muttered, getting out of his car. "Ted, put the man down. I can take it from here."

Ted set the man down and pushed him against the Charger.

Chief London handcuffed the suspect and led him back to his cruiser. He reached in the man's back pocket and extracted his wallet. Studying the license, he confirmed the man was Ray Russo.

"Easiest arrest ever," the chief said under his breath.

Ray protested in his New Jersey accent. "I want a lawyer."

Two other police cars arrived, including a state cop. The men climbed out and rushed to the scene. The chief said, "I have this under control. The FBI wants this man."

"Okay," the officers said and left.

The chief walked over to Ted and asked, "What happened?"

Ted answered, in his thick Hoosier twang, "Gladys and Al were standin' on the sidewalk yellin' at this dude. I thought it was because the city slicker had parked in Al's parking spot. You know ever since Al got his truck back from bein' stolen, he's real particular about his spot," Ted digressed.

"Then what happened?" the chief coached.

"I pulled over to see if I could help. That's when my cat jumped out of the truck and ran over to that dude—"

"Ray Russo," the chief interjected.

"Yeah, him. That SOB tried to kick my cat. And there ain't a person on this planet who kicks my cat and lives to tell about it!"

"Is your cat okay?"

"Hell, yeah. Or you'd be scoopin' a dead man off of the sidewalk."

"Where's your cat now?" the chief asked patiently.

"He's over there. Mouser!" he called.

The rotund ginger cat waddled over and yowled.

"Git in the truck," Ted said.

Mouser raced to the pickup, and with a leap worthy of a gymnast, jumped in through the open window on the passenger side.

"Yep, Chief. He's doin' just fine."

Gladys and Al walked over. "Chief, we want to say how happy we are to see you back on the job. We were so worried about you."

"Thank you both, and Gladys keep up the good work. I really appreciate it."

Gladys smiled from ear to ear. Al put his arm around her and walked her across the street.

Chapter Twenty-Four

Saying Goodbye at the Wind Turbines

A black, government-issued sedan drove down the access lane to the wind turbines on Stevie's property. It parked behind Stevie's Dodge Ram.

Stevie leaned against the tailgate and wore a resigned, solemn expression on his face. Inside his truck, a playful black kitten was batting a belled-ball in her cat carrier.

Two FBI agents got out of the sedan. One walked over to Stevie, "Sir, I need to frisk you."

Stevie held up his arms and patiently waited while the agent did his search. The agent glanced in Stevie's truck and spotted the cat carrier. The kitten mewed.

"Okay," he said to the second agent who opened the door for Rachael. She climbed out, ran to Stevie and fell in his arms.

Out of respect for the couple's privacy, the agents stood a respectful twenty feet away from them.

Stevie tenderly kissed her, then hugged her. "Hey, good lookin'," he said.

"I only have a few minutes," she said. "I came to say good-bye."

"Good-bye until the trial is over, or good-bye forever?" he asked, brushing a strand of hair across her forehead.

"Forever good-bye," she choked. "Oh, Stevie, I fell in love with you the first time I saw you. I never counted on hurting you."

Stevie stood back and looked at her. "Don't worry about me. It ain't gonna be the first time I've fallen off at the rodeo." He hugged her, then asked, "Would you like to say good-bye to Intruder? She's in the truck."

"My heart is breaking now. I can't take any more heartache. Promise me, Stevie, that you and Salina will give her a good home?"

"We will," Stevie's voice broke.

"I'm sorry I didn't tell you about the flash drive, about the mob, about Ray's involvement in it. I just wanted you to see me for who I am. I'm not a bad person. I'm just someone who made a stupid, spur-of-the-moment mistake that I couldn't fix."

"I understand."

"I'm going to testify against the mob. I've been accepted in the Witness Protection Program. Once I'm settled in my new life, I can't contact you."

"I understand that, too," he said sadly.

"It wouldn't be safe for me to come back to Erie. Not for me, you or Salina. The mob would never let me live."

One of the agents coughed nervously and glanced at his watch. "Ms. Thomas, we need to leave. We have a flight to catch."

Stevie grabbed Rachael into another embrace and kissed her again. He whispered in her ear, "I love you. No matter how hard it gets for you, I'm here, thinking about you. I'll never forget you."

Rachael clung to him and cried, then she broke away. One of the agents escorted her back to the car. Rachael climbed into the back seat. The same agent sat next to her. The second one got behind the wheel and put the car in gear.

Stevie sadly watched the sedan as it drove away. Once the vehicle was out of sight, he climbed in his truck and drove home.

Intruder mewed a sweet meow.

"Goin' home, little girl. Goin' home."

Chapter Twenty-Five

Two Weeks Later at the Pink Mansion

Salina sat cross-legged on Katherine's parlor floor. She held a black kitten on her lap. The kitten had finally settled down after running up and down the stairs and climbing the heavy, velvet draperies on some of the windows.

Scout and Abra met the 'new cat in town' with bored expressions on their brown masks. They jumped up to the windowsill and turned their backs to the group. Abby sniffed the kitten, then pawed Salina's bag to see if she could steal anything. "Abby, let's not do that," Katherine scolded. The Abyssinian gave an innocent look and trotted out of the room. Dewey and Crowie wanted to wrestle the kitten, but Katherine nixed that idea. "You guys are too big." The seal-point brothers hiked up their tails and raced upstairs. Lilac me-yowled loudly and also exited the room. But Iris trotted over and began washing Intruder's ears.

"Aww," Katherine cooed. "Iris, good girl," she praised.

Salina said, "I think that went well."

Katherine giggled. "Yes, Part One of kitten meets seven cats."

"I want them to get along so I can bring Intruder over for play time."

"Sounds like I need to buy another cozy bed," then Katherine changed the topic, "How's your dad doing?"

"You mean since *that* woman left."

"Salina, play nice."

"Don't get me started." She frowned.

"You didn't answer my question. How's he handling things?"

"He's all right. He mopes about the house, but has been keeping himself very busy."

"I wonder what will happen with the storefront?"

"Oh, I forgot to tell you. Rachael gave it to dad. He plans on selling it."

"Probably a good idea."

"Oh, here's something else, before I forget it. Rachael left you something." Salina set the kitten on the floor, then reached into her bag. She drew out an envelope and handed it to Katherine. "I've been meaning to deliver this to you."

"What is it?"

"After Rachael left, I found it in the guest room on the dresser. It's addressed to you."

Katherine opened it and quickly scanned the contents. Writing in a flowing cursive, Rachael described her job with the magician, how long she worked for him, and her relationship with Scout and Abra. She wrote several endearing accounts of the Siamese, and how much she loved them. She mentioned that when the magician was performing in the Catskills, she'd take the pair to stay with her grandmother who owned a big, Victorian house in Nyack, New York. She ended the letter by admitting she wanted to take them away from the abusive magician but someone else beat her to it. She was heartbroken when the Siamese sisters were separated, but thrilled that Katherine had ended up with both of them. At the end of the page was a smiley face. "Thank you for everything."

Salina interrupted, "Why don't you read it out loud."

"Oh, it's just a sweet thank you from Rachael." Katherine avoided mentioning the magician's name in front of her sensitive seal-point girls.

Scout and Abra jumped to the floor, stretched, then bolted out of the room. Intruder raced after them in hot pursuit.

Salina giggled. "I better get her. I think she's had enough excitement for the day."

Salina wrangled the kitten down the stairs, then said, "I'm leaving now."

"Thanks for coming. Say hello to your dad."

Salina put the kitten over her shoulder, picked up her bag, and left.

As Katherine was closing the door, Chief London pulled up in front of the mansion. Katherine met him halfway. "I'm so happy to see you. How are you doing?"

"Better every day," he said. "Bruised ribs are not any fun."

"Oh, how I know. Been there, done that," Katherine agreed. "Come in. I have something to return to you."

"I think I know what it is."

They walked inside the house. Katherine led the chief to the living room where Iris eyed him curiously.

He spoke to the Siamese. "Glad to see you. I don't have anything of interest in my pockets, but you can check anyway."

Iris yowled excitedly.

The chief sat down on the damask loveseat.

Katherine walked to the marble-topped curio and lifted the chief's photo of his wife and returned it to him. "Iris would like to apologize for stealing this from you."

The chief tipped his head back and laughed. "As soon as I discovered it was gone, I knew the thief had taken it. What do you have to say for yourself?" he asked Iris.

Iris didn't answer but jumped up on his lap. She reached up and tapped his short-cropped beard with her paw. The chief rubbed her ears. Iris was cross-eyed in cat heaven and purred loudly.

Katherine asked, "Have you heard anything about Rachael Thomas?"

"Only that she's testifying against the kingpin of the mob, who ran a money laundering website. His name is Marcel Blumberg, and his colleague is Ray Russo."

"Wow, if I was Rachael, I'd be scared to death."

"I can imagine she is. You heard the news about Stevie?"

"Sort of. What news?"

"Rachael gave him the storefront and a Tercel."

"Salina just told me about the storefront but not about the old car."

"You know I'm not superstitious, but I think that place has some bad karma associated with it."

"Because of what happened to you and Officer Troy?"

"Yep."

"Could be. I wonder who'll buy it?"

"I hope someone local."

Katherine snickered. "Someone local and not connected to the mob?"

"That's about right." The chief gently removed Iris from his lap. "I better be off. I told the Missus I'd come home for lunch, so I best be going."

Katherine became serious. "Jake and I are so happy you're okay."

"Me, too," he said, brushing off the sentiment. "Oh, and Katz, next time I have a suspect, can I bring 'em over here, so your cats can help me search for evidence?"

"Well, not thinking that's a great idea. I'm kind of hoping the cats are going through a phase."

"Ha!" he belted. "Habitual cat criminals. I knew it!" The chief headed to the door and left.

Katherine climbed the stairs to check on the cats. She counted her lucky stars that the chief was wearing a bulletproof vest. She trembled to think about what a tragic loss it would have been if he'd been killed. She felt sorry for Rachael and even sorrier for Stevie. She hoped someday he'd find the right one.

Suddenly, in the midst of gloomy thoughts, she was overcome with happiness, as if a ray of sunshine had broken through a cloudy day. She was happy in her marriage, happy with her friends, and happy with her extraordinary cats that were special in more ways than one.

Dear Reader . . .

Thank you so much for reading my book. Many of you emailed and asked me to write more about the other cats, besides Scout and Abra. Well, I hope I've done this in *The Cats that Cooked the Books*.

Coincidences are a common occurrence. Just the other day, I drove into the city and literally bumped into three cousins I hadn't seen in years. I'm sure you can think of dozens of coincidences as well. It's a normal part of life.

I love it when my readers write to me. I try to answer all emails within twenty-four hours.

Email me at: karenannegolden@gmail.com

For all of you, who will write reviews on Amazon and/or Goodreads, thank you so much. I very much appreciate it.

I love to post pictures of my cats on my Facebook pages, and would enjoy learning about your pets as well. Follow me @ https://www.facebook.com/karenannegolden

If you are new to the series, the following pages describe my other books. If you love mysteries with cats, don't miss these action-packed page turners.

Thanks again.

Karen

The Cats that Surfed the Web

Book One in *The Cats that . . . Cozy Mystery series*

If you haven't read the first book, *The Cats that Surfed the Web*, you can download the Kindle or paperback version on Amazon.

The Cats that Surfed the Web, is an action-packed, exhilarating read. When Katherine "Katz" Kendall, a career woman with cats, discovers she's the sole heir of a huge inheritance, she can't believe her good luck. She's okay with the conditions in the will: Move from New York City to the small town of Erie, Indiana, live in her great aunt's pink Victorian mansion, and take care of an Abyssinian cat. With her three Siamese cats and best friend Colleen riding shotgun, Katz leaves Manhattan to find a former housekeeper dead in the basement. There are people in the town who are furious that they didn't get the money. But who would be greedy enough to get rid of the rightful heir to take the money and run?

Four adventurous felines help Katz solve the crimes by mysteriously "searching" the Internet for clues. If you love cats, especially cozy cat mysteries, you'll enjoy this series.

The Cats that Chased the Storm

Book Two in *The Cats that* . . . Cozy Mystery series

It's early May in Erie, Indiana, and the weather has turned most foul. We find Katherine "Katz" Kendall, heiress to the Colfax fortune, living in a pink mansion, caring for her three Siamese and Abby the Abyssinian. Severe thunderstorms frighten the cats, but Scout is better than any weather app. A different storm is brewing, however, with a discovery that connects great-uncle William Colfax to the notorious gangster John Dillinger. Why is the Erie Historical Society so eager to get William's personal papers? Is the new man in Katherine's life a fortune hunter? Will Abra mysteriously reappear, and is Abby a magnet for danger?

A fast-paced whodunit, the second book in "The Cats that" series involves four extraordinary felines that help Katz unravel the mysteries in her life.

The Cats that Told a Fortune

Book Three in *The Cats that* . . . Cozy Mystery series

In the land of corn mazes and covered bridge festivals, a serial killer is on the loose. Autumn in Erie, Indiana means cool days of intrigue and subterfuge. Katherine "Katz" Kendall settles into her late great aunt's Victorian mansion with her five cats. A Halloween party at the mansion turns out to be more than Katz planned for. Meanwhile, she's teaching her first computer training class, and a serial killer is murdering young women. Along the way, Katz and her cats uncover important clues to the identity of the killer, and find out about Erie's local crime family . . . the hard way.

The Cats that Played the Market

Book Four in *The Cats that . . .* Cozy Mystery series

  A blizzard blows into Indiana, bringing gifts, gala events, and a ghastly murder to heiress Katherine "Katz" Kendall. It's Katherine's birthday, and she gets more than she bargains for when someone evil from her past comes back to haunt her. After all hell breaks loose at the Erie Museum's opening, Katherine and her five cats unwittingly stumble upon clues that help solve a mystery. But has Scout lost her special abilities? Or will Katz find that another one of her amazing felines is a super-sleuth?

  With the cats providing clues, it's up to Katherine and her friends to piece together the murderous puzzle . . . before the town goes bust!

The Cats that Watched the Woods

Book Five in *The Cats that . . .* Cozy Mystery series

What have the extraordinary cats of millionaire Katherine "Katz" Kendall surfed up now? "Idyllic vacation cabin by a pond stocked with catfish." It's July in Erie, Indiana, and steamy weather fuels the tension between Katz and her fiancé, Jake. Katz rents the cabin for a private getaway, though Siamese cats, Scout and Abra, demand to go along. How does a peaceful, serene setting go south in such a hurry? Is the terrifying man in the woods real, or is he the legendary ghost of Peace Lake? It's up to Katz and her cats to piece together the mysterious puzzle. The fifth book in the popular "The Cats that . . . Cozy Mystery" series is a suspenseful, thrilling ride that will keep you on the edge of your seat.

The Cats that Stalked a Ghost

Book Six in *The Cats that* . . . Cozy Mystery series

While Katherine and Jake are tying the knot at her pink mansion, a teen ghost has other plans, which shake their Erie, Indiana town to its core. How does a beautiful September wedding end in mistaken identity . . . and murder? What does an abandoned insane asylum have to do with a spirit that is haunting Katz? Colleen, a paranormal investigator at night and student by day, shows Katz how to communicate with ghosts. An arsonist is torching historic properties. Will the mansion be his next target? Ex-con Stevie Sanders and the Siamese play their own stalking games, but for different reasons. It's up to Katz and her extraordinary felines to solve two mysteries: one hot, one cold. Seal-point Scout wants a new adventure fix, and litter-mate Abra fetches a major clue that puts an arsonist behind bars.

The Cats that Stole a Million

Book Seven in *The Cats that* . . . Cozy Mystery series

  Millionaire Katherine, aka Katz, husband Jake and their seven cats return to the pink mansion after the explosion wreaked havoc several months earlier. Now the house has been restored, will it continue to be a murder magnet? Erie, Indiana is crime-free for the first time since heiress Katherine, aka Katz, and her cats moved into town. Everyone is at peace until domestic harmony is disrupted by an uninvited visitor from Brooklyn. Why is Katz's friend being tracked by a NYC mob? Meanwhile, ex-con Stevie Sanders wants to go clean, but ties to dear old Dad (Erie's notorious crime boss) keep pulling him back. Murder, lies, and a million-dollar theft have Katz and her seven extraordinary cats working on borrowed time to unravel a mystery.

The Cats that Broke the Spell

Book Eight in *The Cats that . . .* Cozy Mystery series

When a beautiful professor is accused of being a witch, she retreats to her cabin in the woods. Soon a man dressed like a scarecrow begins to stalk her, and vandals leave pentagrams at her front gate. The town of Erie, Indiana has never known a witch hunt, but after the first accusation, the news spreads like wildfire. "She stole another woman's husband, then murdered him," people raged in the local diner. "She uses her black cats to cast spells to do her evil deeds!" But what do the accusers really want? How is Erie's crime boss involved? In the meantime, while the pink mansion's attic is being remodeled, Katz, Jake and their seven felines move out to a rural farmhouse, which is next door to the "witch." They find themselves drawn into a deadly conflict on several fronts. It's up to Katz and her seven extraordinary cats to unravel the tangle of lies before mass hysteria wrecks the town. Murder, mayhem, and a cold case make this book a thrilling, action-packed read that will keep you guessing until the very end.

The Cats that Stopped the Magic

Book Nine in *The Cats that . . .* Cozy Mystery series

This classic whodunit boasts a new cast of characters: a self-centered magician, a compulsive gambler, a sweet cat wrangler and her grandmother, a caring nurse, and a wealthy couple. How are their lives intertwined with a show cat named Abra? In 2009, two Siamese cats performed in Magic Harry's Hocus-Pocus show, in front of hundreds of devoted fans. But their lives were far from magical, and their careers were cut short when Abra was stolen backstage after a performance. Why did the magician increase the insurance on Abra days before she disappeared? Was Abra stolen and sold on the black market? Or did anonymous cat-lovers rescue her from a life-threatening situation? A wealthy tycoon wants a Siamese cat with a specific look for his dying wife. Why? Four years later, Abra ends up in an animal shelter. Where had she been during this time? Back in Erie, Indiana, Katherine and Jake work on borrowed time to piece the puzzle together before Magic Harry tries to take Abra away from them.

The Cats that Walked the Haunted Beach

Book Ten in *The Cats that . . .* Cozy Mystery series

This fast-paced mystery is chock-full of coincidences and bizarre twists. When Colleen and Daryl get together to plan their wedding, they can't agree on anything. Colleen is at her wits' end. Best friend Katherine votes for a time-out and proposes a girls' retreat to a town named Seagull, which borders Lake Michigan and the famous Indiana dunes. Mum is adamant they stay in a rented cabin right on the beach. Against Katz's better judgment, she agrees with Mum's plan — only on one condition: she's bringing Scout and Abra, who become very upset when she's away from them. With the Siamese in tow, Katherine and Colleen head to the dunes to find that Mum's weekend retreat is far from ideal. The first night, they have a paranormal experience and learn that a ghost walks the beach when someone is going to be murdered. Meanwhile, ex-con Stevie has a date with a woman he met online. But this news doesn't prevent the town gossips from spreading a rumor that he's having an affair with a married woman. How does Abra finding a wallet lead to a mix-up with dangerous consequences? It's up to Katz and her extraordinary cats to unravel a deadly plot that ends in murder.

Acknowledgements

I wish to thank my husband, Jeff Dible, who edited the first draft of this book. Thanks for supporting my creative process and helping me clarify complicated plot points.

Thank you, Vicki Braun, for being my amazing editor. You've been there for me on ten of my books. You are the best.

Also, thanks to Rob Williams, my book cover artist. I'm always impressed how you can incorporate four or more stock photos into a seamless picture.

Thanks, Ramona and Louie for beta reading my book.

Thanks to my loyal readers, my family, and friends.

The Cats that . . . Cozy Mystery series would never be without the input from my furry friends. My husband and I have many cats, ranging in ages from five to sixteen-years-old.

Printed in Great Britain
by Amazon